Title: Sacred Thorn
Subtitle: Collection Book for Hot Romance Short Stories
Author: Vivian Logan

AF440075

This is a work of fiction. Any resemblance to any person, living or dead is purely coincidental.

From the Publisher:
Thank you for purchasing this book.

Table of Contents

His Secret Life

Description

While walking through a dark alley, Casey gets an unsettling feeling, which she dismisses until a disgruntled admirer confronts her. Luckily, she is rescued by a stranger with unforgettable eyes.

Two weeks later, she accepts a job as a night shift receptionist at a motel, but on her first day, she makes a terrible mistake. This mistake reveals a scary secret that Casey is threatened with keeping. She is not so easily swayed, though, especially after identifying her rescuer.

Determined to repay the favor, Casey aids Kenneth, her new boss, and diligently nurses him back to health. This leads to a romantic revelation and a passionate night of lovemaking. But drama follows the couple the following night when Kenneth's former clan leader takes them. There, Kenneth challenges Levi in a match which he heroically wins, earning them their freedom, but this victory also comes with a surprising position.

Chapter 1

"I'm almost there," Casey spoke through her cellular phone as her footsteps echoed through the alley, cutting through the stillness of the night.

The streets were mostly empty now, but hours before, it was bustling with shopping tourists. However, as soon as the sun went down, they fled to their accommodations, leaving the streets to the locals looking for a night of fun.

"I'm going through the alley now. See you in a bit," she told the person on the other end of the phone before ending the call.

Casey walked briskly through the small space, diverting the garbage thrown out by the store owners. The alley was dark, with limited lights at the ends joining the main streets.

As she passed the cluster of cardboard boxes, she stopped and eyed the area behind her where she had just come through. Casey couldn't help having the feeling she was being watched. It was a tingling sensation that created a queasiness in her stomach and put her on edge.

Though she saw no one, the feeling remained, tying her stomach in knots.

Casey shook her head and continued on her path, speeding up her pace to the bar. She had been stressing about not finding a job recently. Maybe it was playing on her mind. Nevertheless, she was relieved when she approached the building with loitering couples and loud music emanating from the inside.

"Casey. Casey. Over here."

Casey scanned the room for where her friend was calling and found her at the far corner with her hand waving wildly in the air. Lil was dressed in a long-sleeved top with extremely short denim shorts. She paired this with black thigh-high boots and flashy accessories that matched her personality. When

Casey met Lil, she was a brunette, but since then had become a blonde and now a fiery redhead.

Usually the center of attention, Lil was accustomed to getting her way and sometimes took the privileged act too far. Nevertheless, Casey loved her. She was the first friend Casey met when she moved five years ago, and since then, they had become inseparable.

"What's up, Lil," Casey greeted her friend, taking the seat beside her.

Next to Lil, Casey's outfit was considered boring. She wore dark blue jeans distressed at the knees and a sleeveless top. On her feet were dark brown strapped heeled sandals that matched her side bag with the long strap. Her makeup was kept natural and the only jewelry she wore was a circular gold stud.

Casey wrapped her blonde hair in a ponytail on top of her head and folded it at the ends. During the day she hide behind dark sunglasses but as darkness rolled in, she tucked them into her bag.

"What took you so long?" Lil took one of the shots and placed it in front of Casey.

"My interview went a little long," Cassey told her, breathing out hard. "The manager wanted to know every detail of my life."

"So you got it then," Lil's eyes opened wide, and she sat at the edge of the chair with expectation.

Casey shook her head and wrapped her hand around the glass. "No. He said I wasn't what he was looking for."

Lil released a series of obscenities, followed by speculations about the manager's choice in women.

"Don't worry, Casey," she said when she calmed down. "You'll find something soon."

Casey kept her head down and let her friend's reassuring words float past her.

"Oh, I'll be right back," Lil stood suddenly. "I had a few drinks before you came and I think they're ready to come out." Lil squeezed her thighs together and disappeared into the crowd in the washroom's direction.

Left alone to reflect on her failed interview, Casey tossed her head back and gulped down the shot. However, a deep voice almost caused her to choke.

"Mind if I join you?" The man that spoke wore a light blue shirt and dark trousers. He was big, but not quite muscular. and sported a rugged beard.

Casey pointed in the direction Lil had disappeared. "I already have company. She'll be back any minute."

"I saw that friend of yours," the man said. "She can't satisfy you the way I can."

Casey jerked her head back at the man's shocking comment. "Is this your idea of picking up women?" she asked.

The man kept his body upright, holding her gaze. "I'm simply stating the facts."

Casey was usually polite and composed, and it took more than a little forwardness to get her rattled. She leaned back in the seat. "Well, thanks for the information, but I don't need satisfying. I'm pretty content."

The man narrowed his eyes and adopted a rigid posture. "Why don't you think it over?" he asked in a low, rumbling tone. "You might regret it."

Casey smiled then. Her forehead was wrinkled. "I assure you I won't."

"If you say so," he retorted before walking away.

Long after the man left, Casey still couldn't shake that eerie feeling that lingered around their conversation. The glint in his eyes also rattled her insides.

"Are you ready for a fun night?" the words came from behind and Casey squinted at her friend's voice. "See. This is exactly what I'm talking about," Lil said as she reclaimed her seat. "You need to drink, relax, and have fun."

That was exactly what the women did, but at the end of the night, Lil was the one completely intoxicated. Casey called her friend a cab, told the driver her address, and took the driver's information. Then she staggered lower down the street to get a bus. It was already late but being jobless did not allow Casey such luxuries as to hire two taxis in one night. Lil's cab fare alone had sent her night's budget over the edge, so she decided that no matter the time, she would wait for the bus.

Casey was the only one around when she felt it again. The same eerie feeling that caused the tiny hairs on her hand to become erect. It was a feeling that unsettled her at her core, so she pushed herself off the bus stop bench and track a route to the bar she had left when a man suddenly intercepted her path, gazing at her with malice.

Casey altered her direction to walk around him, but the man made it impossible for her to pass. She took a step back and stared up at his face instead, recognizing his twisted lip immediately.

"Can you please get out of my way?" Casey pushed out her chest and held her chin high. She was trying hard not to show her fear.

"Where's your friend now?" The man growled before looking around. "Seems like she abandoned you."

"She did not abandon me. She just went around the corner for something." Casey gripped the strap of her bag tighter.

The man opened his eyes wide and tilted his chin. "Is that right? Cause I could have sworn it was her I saw getting into that sedan earlier."

Casey took a step back then, her heart speeding at an alarming rate.

"You know what I think," the man decreased the distance between them. "I think you're all alone."

He reached out to her and caught her shoulder as Casey screamed and tried to free herself.

She was still tugging in his arms when a booming voice caused both of them to turn sharply.

"Let her go." The stranger approached them slowly with his hand in his pocket. He stood with his body tall, not that he needed any extra height. He was easily a foot taller than Casey.

She eyed him from head to toe. Taking in his curly dark brown hair and uniquely green eyes. This man's face was covered in facial hair, giving him a rugged but sexy look. Though the situation was not suited for it, Casey felt the shudders in her loins and turned her head.

"Mind your business, man, and you won't get hurt." Casey's attacker was still holding on to her.

The handsome stranger that was awakening her sensitivity stopped in front of them. "If you walk away now, maybe I'll allow you to keep your legs."

Casey's attacker gave the stranger a hateful glare and cackled before his expression suddenly changed. His mouth fell open and at the same time, his eyes widened and his grip loosened.

"What the hell are you?" were his last words before he turned and bolted out of sight. Casey kept her eyes on him until he disappeared.

"You shouldn't walk the streets alone at this hour." She turned around to take in the stranger's pronounced jawline. Being this close to him now was almost intoxicating.

Casey swallowed hard. "Thank you," she said, but the man was already walking away.

Chapter 2

Casey lifted her feet high to cross the threshold lined with buckets to catch the leaking water. The lobby of the motel was small, but at least it wasn't completely dilapidated, like some of the others she had been to.

"Hello." Casey walked up to the man at the front desk to get his attention. Though her arrival was not quite, the man didn't bother to raise his head from the newspaper. "I have an interview with Mr. Lessey."

The man turned around then and took in her appearance. She was wearing dark blue jeans with a pink t-shirt and sneakers. Her makeup was light and her hair was pulled into a low ponytail. Casey believed she had dressed appropriately for the interview but as beady eyes scanned her, doubts filled her head.

Casey clutched the strap of her bag. "Do you know where I can find him?"

"That would be me," the man said, folding his newspaper and swinging himself around on the chair. "Did you bring your resume?"

"Yes, I did." Casey dug into her bag and produced the white envelope, offering it to her interviewer.

The man scanned the pages of the document while Casey shifted from one foot to another. "Are you comfortable working night shifts?"

Casey took in a breath and held it. The truth was that she was not. She hated staying up all night, but if she wanted to keep her apartment, she needed a job as soon as possible.

"Yes, I am," Casey lied and fisted her hand at her back in hopes that her interviewer would not notice the twitching of her jaw.

The man looked up from the documents she handed him. "Can you start immediately?"

Casey swallowed hard as a small smile curled her lips. "Sure. That is not a problem."

"One last thing. You would also be expected to perform some personal assistant duties to the owner. He has certain... requests to be done every twenty-nine to thirty days. It is very important that you follow these instructions exactly." The man spoke with intense eyes, willing her to acknowledge the seriousness of his words.

Casey nodded in acknowledgment. "What do I have to do?"

The man lowered his eyes. "Nothing difficult. Starting tonight, at seven, lock his room from the outside and whatever you do, do not go in."

Casey's eyelashes fluttered rapidly, but the rest of her body remained unfazed. She wanted to enquire about the strange task but had a feeling she wouldn't get an answer even if she did, so she kept her questions to herself. "Understood."

"Great," the man said, scooped up his newspaper, and made his way out of the receptionist area. "Everything else is straightforward. When someone comes in, you take their money and give them a key. The rates of the rooms are on the counter. You also have to record everything in the notebook."

Casey scanned the area, her eyes landing on the laminated sheet taped to the countertop. "Ok."

Before the man left the building, he said. "I will be back to relieve you in the morning. Don't forget to lock the door."

"I won't," Casey said, entering the small receptionist's area.

Casey scanned her surroundings. Keys lined the wall, each one attached to a numbered tag. Some slots were missing a key and Casey assumed they were the rooms that were already filled.

She flipped open the notebook to the last used page. Lines were drawn from top to bottom to create columns, each one requiring different information. Then she snapped the book closed and dropped herself onto the chair, breathing out hard.

"It's not the best situation," she said, noting the faded paint on the walls. "But it will do for now."

Sighing, she took out her phone and stored her bag in the cupboard below. Then she texted her best friend informing her of her job status. Lil didn't respond, so Casey stuffed her headphones in her ear and turned on the music. No one entered the building after her and before long she was consumed by the musical tracks of Avril Lavigne.

It was the rumbling of her stomach that snapped Casey out of her pop-rock trace as her eyes went to the clock on the wall. Her head jerked back immediately and her eyes widened as she discovered her first on-the-job mistake. Without haste, Casey bolted from her seat and dashed towards the door that Mr. Lessey had pointed to when speaking of the owner. She scurried down the hallway, almost tripping on her feet, and collided with the door, knocking her shoulder slightly.

Casey moaned and rubbed the tender area before reaching for the two rim locks and the three-barrel bolts attached to the door. It was then that she heard it. Low grunting sounds much like her own, but more intense.

Her body froze as she recalled Mr. Lessey's instructions. "Do not go in." He gave her that warning for a reason, but how could she ignore the pained sounds coming from the inside? What if the owner of the motel was hurt and in need of assistance? She couldn't just stand outside, knowing that she might be able to do something to help. So instead of following instructions on her first day of work, Casey pushed open the metal door and barged into the room, but the sight that greeted her was far from what she expected.

Standing in the middle of the sitting room was a man, only he didn't quite look like a man. His ears were erect, but it was not as pronounced as the nose that extended from his face. The man's fingers were replaced with claws and his body was covered with overgrown hair. Casey stood frozen, her heart beating rapidly and eyes widened as the man's canine teeth extended beyond what was considered normal.

A gasp escaped her then, and it seemed to capture the man's attention. He turned towards her, eyes a brilliant yellow, and roared in a half animalistic voice. "Get out of here now."

Though her mind was still in a daze, her body sprang back into action then, as she turned abruptly and scampered out. Casey slammed the door shut behind her, locking it with shaky hands and a rapid breath. Then she slowly backed away, not willing to accept what she had seen.

Chapter 3

Fragments of the night occupied Casey's thoughts throughout the following day. She couldn't quite comprehend what she saw, but she knew it wasn't natural and it definitely wasn't something she should have seen.

"How am I supposed to go to that place again?" Casey spoke to herself in the mirror as she dressed for her shift. She felt as if her mind was asleep and her body was simply going through the motions.

Great! At least this way she would be detached from whatever happened on her shift.

Casey kept that mentality as she walked into the lobby, her eyes wondering wildly at the paintings on the wall.

"What the hell did you do last night?" Mr. Lessey caused the weight of her feet to halt all their movement.

"What do you mean?" Casey stammered while clutching her bag. She knew exactly what she did, enter the owner's room, yet she pretended to be clueless. Maybe if she denied it, she wouldn't be forced to recall the frightful sight that prevented her from closing her eyes the entire day.

"I don't know what you did, but he's pissed." The 'he,' Mr. Lessey was referring to, was obviously the owner of the motel. "He asked me to send you to his apartment the moment you came in today."

Casey swallowed hard, her voice shaky. "He wants me to go in there?" She pointed to the room, numbered 101.

"That's what I said, didn't I? Just make it quick and return to your post as soon as possible. I'm leaving as soon as the clock strikes seven." Mr. Lessey turned away from her then, blocking his face with the day's newspaper, which signified the end of their conversation.

Casey sighed, her stomach in turmoil and her face ashen.

"The longer you wait, the more pissed he's going to become. My advice is to just get it over with." The man spoke without looking away from the newspaper.

Casey took a deep breath and willed her feet down the corridor, where she knocked on the door, she had scampered out of just the night before. Her hand was shaking, but it seemed to freeze when the deep masculine voice on the other side of the door said, "Come in."

With wavering steps, she entered the apartment, surprised by what she saw. The night before, she was too taken aback to pay attention to anything but the morphing figure in the middle of the room, a room which she now appreciated for its intricate design.

Casey was expecting a bachelor pad, maybe a lazy boy couch, and a large screen television but as she looked around then, she couldn't even spot the entertainment electronic. There was, however, a large bookshelf laden with the reading materials. Next to it was a single couch with a side table to its right. On that table was a lamp and three hardcover books. It was close to the window with burglar-proof bars sporting clusters of indentations. Besides the single couch, there were two others, both covered with sheets.

"Have a seat." Casey dropped into the closest couch as soon as she heard the deep rumbling. She had almost forgotten her situation until her boss spoke. His body turned away from her to stare at an open window.

"Do you know who I am?" Her boss kept his tone indifferent and his posture relaxed.

"You're the owner of this motel. Kenneth." Casey kept her hands in her lap, nervously entwining her fingers together.

"Yes, I am," the man said, his hand in his pocket. "And as your boss, I constructed rules. Rules that you broke on your first night here."

Casey kept her head low but said nothing. She was waiting for the wrath she was certain would follow.

"The rules were simple." Kenneth raked his hand through his curly, dark brown hair. "Lock the door and do not enter under any circumstances."

"I heard a noise, and I thought you might have been in trouble." Casey allowed her voice to flow across the room, but she was unsure if it reached his ears.

"What did you see?" The man's shoulder was stiffening with tension.

"I... I didn't see anything," Casey said, her voice rattling.

Kenneth obviously didn't believe her since his voice became harsh, his swift movement as he turned around startling Casey. "If you tell anyone what you saw here last night, I will come after you. Do you understand me?"

Casey's eyes were closed, but she nodded her response.

"Open your eyes and answer me with words. I need to make sure you understand me and do as I say this time," came the harsh command.

Her eyes opened then to unique green ones. Casey had seen eyes like that only two weeks ago when a stranger saved her from a man outside the bar.

Those eyes weren't hostile. They weren't the eyes of someone with the slightest aggressiveness, but they were defensive. Casey held Kenneth's gaze and for a moment, they both said nothing as the tension left her body, washing her with relief.

"It was you, wasn't it?" Her legs suddenly gained strength, and she stood, inches away from the man who just threatened her. "It was you who saved me close to the bar that night."

Kenneth swallowed hard and turned away from her, his hands fidgeting. "I don't know what you're talking about."

It was an obvious lie.

"You stopped that guy from harassing me two weeks ago," she said in a low, amusing tone.

Kenneth's words were harsh now, but Casey didn't believe he intended to hurt her at all. He was just putting on an act so that she wouldn't tell others about what she saw.

Though Casey wasn't even sure of what happened the night before, she wouldn't tell anyone. How could she endanger someone who had saved her?

"You risked your life to save me that night, but I never got a chance to thank you. So, I am thanking you now." Casey turned to leave, but before she did, she left Kenneth with reassuring words. "And you don't have to worry. I wouldn't say anything to anyone about what I saw here last night."

Chapter 4

Casey returned to the receptionist's desk, but every so often her eyes darted to the door to Kenneth's apartment. She had called his bluff, and he was completely stunned, reassuring her she was right. Kenneth never intended to harm her, only scare her in keeping his secret. A secret she had no intention of revealing.

The door opened, signaling the first guest of the night, but it wasn't the crowd Casey was expecting. The night before occupants of the motel room was mainly coupled. Couples of all sorts, but couples. But these first guest was a group of well-built men. Three followed the lead of a bald, rugged man and even dusted the drops of rain from his jacket as he entered.

Casey followed them with narrowed eyes until they stopped at her desk. The bald one pierced her with his eyes, his jaw twitching, but it wasn't him that spoke. "We are here to see Kenneth."

She looked from one to the other, then rested on the leader. These were definitely not guests; she was certain of it. And even more certain, they would cause nothing but trouble.

"Is he expecting you?" She stood erect and kept her voice steady, unwilling to show these men the slightest hint she was unsure of herself. Her boss had defended her and she would do her best to repay the favor.

"We don't need an appointment," minion number one said. "Just point us in the right direction."

Casey turned her gaze from the subordinate to the leader. She lifted her chin and stood tall. "I'm sorry I can't do that. Why don't you give me your names and I will check if he can see you?"

"Why you little..." the minion began, but the rising of the boss' hand quickly cut him off.

"You must not know who I am, but I can assure you, I am not someone who you want to mess with. I can make your entire life vanish with just a single bite." The bald man peeled back his lip to reveal extended canines.

Casey gasp. Her hand flew up to her chest, trying to calm her racing heart. These men were not completely human in the same way her boss wasn't.

"What do you think you're doing?"

Casey whipped her head around at the sound of a familiar voice. Her boss was standing at his doorway, his hand folded into a fist with furious eyes directed at her. "How dare you refuse my guests?"

"I'm sorry but..." Casey dropped her hand, her breathing somewhat regulating in Kenneth's presence.

"No buts. In fact, why don't you leave for the rest of the night and we will discuss this in the morning?"

Casey's face fell and her legs were weakening. "But I just started my shift."

"And I just ended it," Kenneth said with some finality. "Now leave before I send you home permanently." Then to his guest, he said. "I am sorry about my receptionist. She is new. Come this way and we will talk."

As the men followed Kenneth into his apartment, Casey didn't miss the smirk that stretched across the bald man's face. "Count yourself lucky," he said and disappeared into the apartment.

Releasing a heavy sigh, Casey allowed her body to drop on the chair as her eyes flickered from her boss' door to where her bag rested in the cupboard. She was instructed to leave, but her intuition urged her to stay. Those men were brimming with hostility and it gave her an uneasiness in her stomach. So Casey lingered around.

She was brainstorming for excuses why she disobeyed jet another instruction, why she remained at her post, when the first set of banging caused her to jump in her seat. It was followed by a series of shattering glass and scuffling. When something heavy hit her boss' door, Casey squealed and clutched to the edge of her desk. The need to enter the apartment was strong, but her legs wouldn't dare take her there. They suffered from a sudden loss of energy.

When the door opened, it was the four men who emerged, their faces bright with laughter. The bald one kept his eyes on her and just before he exited the building, he sent her a kiss and licked his lips. Casey stared at him, wide mouth and slightly shivering. She was only able to move several seconds after the men disappeared.

Only then she was able to rush into the completely ramshackle room. Broken glass from the lamp lay at her feet, next to shards of furniture. Casey took her time navigating through the mess. Four evenly long strokes tore the cushions for the couch, revealing the foam inside. Those two were scattered around the room now, housing a fist-size hole in the wall.

"Kenneth?" Casey called with a choked voice, but it was met with no response. Her heart rate quickened in fear that something had happened to him. The next time she screamed his name, there was an urgency in her voice and she spun around wide, her eyes fluttering to all the corners of the room.

Finally, she noticed a motionless body barely recognizable.

Chapter 5

Casey scampered to the unconscious man, kneeling to roll him over, better assessing his condition.

"Kenneth," she nudged gently. When he didn't respond, he called again in a louder voice, her shakes becoming more frantic.

Kenneth's face was busted, and there was a heavy flow of blood coming from his head. His hand was twisted backward in an unnatural way, certainly broken.

Casey patted her pockets and when her hand rested on her phone, she took it out and dialed a number. "Please don't be dead," she urged as her eyes filled with moisture.

While waiting for the person on the other end of the line to pick up, Casey squeezed her eyelids shut and pressed her free hand to her forehead. There was a lot of tension there and the back of her head was beginning to pain.

"Put down the phone." Casey's eyes flew open to the sound of the weakened voice.

Releasing a held breath, she said, "Don't worry. I'm getting you help." She felt as if a heavy load had been taken off her shoulders.

"No, don't." Kenneth struggled to sit up, sending him into a coughing fit.

Casey kept her gaze on him even as the emergency personnel called to her on the line. Kenneth was seriously hurt, and she didn't understand why he didn't want to go to the hospital. If she didn't get him help, she was certain he would die.

"Please Casey, put down the phone." Kenneth's hand rested on her wrist, causing a tingling and warm sensation.

Casey couldn't help but stare into Kenneth's pleading eyes as she spoke through the phone. "Never mind, he woke up," she said right before she cut off the phone. To him, she said, "I don't know why you didn't want me to call the ambulance, but I trust you."

Kenneth's eyes closed then, and his body seemed to relax. "Can you help me to the couch?"

Casey nodded and angled her hand to give support to Kenneth as he pulled his body upward. His movements were slow, and he moaned and clung to his ribs with every step. When Casey lowered him to the hard surface, he grimaced and the wound at his ribs flowed heavier.

"Tell me what you need," Casey urged as her heart ached from watching him in so much agony.

Kenneth groaned and closed his eyes as he leaned back on the couch. His jaw was tight and there were creases on his forehead. "A washcloth and time."

Casey didn't know about time, but a washcloth she could handle. She rushed into the back and pulled one from the towel rack in the bathroom. When she returned, Kenneth's hand was soaked in blood. Casey paused before rushing to him, applying the cloth to his wound. She pressed hard, using her full force until the heavy flow of blood trickled away. Casey sighed then, as the tension in her shoulders relaxed, though the tightness in her chest did not disappear.

"You have to help me with my arm."

Casey's eyes grew wide as she struggled to decipher her boss' words. "What?"

"My hand is broken. Help me pop it back so that it could heal." Kenneth's voice was a little stronger. "I heal fast, so we need to do it now."

Casey remained in her stooped position. "I can't."

"Yes, you can. Just hold it and pop it back in. Don't worry, I won't feel a thing," Kenneth reassured her, and she slowly took a position to better allow her to complete her task.

When Casey pulled on Kenneth's arm, there was a loud popping sound and he screamed and grind his teeth.

"I thought you said it wouldn't hurt." Casey's voice was high-pitched as she backed away.

Kenneth looked at her. "Would you have done it if I said it would be excruciating?"

He was right, of course. If she knew the extent of his pain, she could have never force herself to reconstruct his hand. Sighing, she lowered her head and willed herself to return to his side. "What do I do now?"

"Now you give me time," Kenneth said, and leaned his head back and closed his eyes. His body became still and Casey hoped he was only sleeping.

With Kenneth incapacitated, Casey took the opportunity to tend to his wounds. Finding scissors was time-consuming, but eventually, she retrieved one from the top draw in his bathroom. Then she used it to cut his shirt off, exposing his broad chest, which sent shivers throughout her body. Shivers that were followed by a loud gasp.

Casey blocked her mouth with her hand, both from shock and to stop herself from screaming. She couldn't believe her eyes, even as she lowered her head to get a closer look at Kenneth's skin pulling together and closing the wound. "What are you?" she whispered, knowing that he could not hear her.

Despite her curiosity and confusion, she silently cleaned Kenneth's wounds, which were looking less severe. Then she went to the kitchen, busying herself. When Kenneth wake, he would need sustenance to help him heal.

She found a parcel of chicken and some vegetables and used it to create a healthy soup. Casey was pouring it into a bowl when she heard him stir.

"You're awake?" Casey said as she brought the bowl with the hot broth to his side. "I made soup for you," she said as

Kenneth pushed himself into a seated position. When he took the bowl from her, he used the hand which had been twisted backward earlier. Casey paused and took a few seconds before relinquishing the bowl.

"Careful. It's hot," she warned as Kenneth took the bowl with his bare hands. Her eyes widened then. Even with mittens on, she still felt the heat from the soup, yet Kenneth held it with ease.

He must have noticed her loose jaw because he said, "Don't worry. I don't burn easily." He took one spoonful and rest the bowl on the table. "Aren't you going to ask?"

Casey tilted her head. "What?"

He held her gaze. "Usually, it's the first thing people want to know. Aren't you curious about what you saw the other night and how I'm healing so quickly?"

Casey kept her head low and toyed with her fingers. "I am," she said softly. "But I thought it might be rude to ask."

Her response caused laughter to erupt from Kenneth. "I knew since I first saw you, you were different." Then he leaned back on the couch, folded his arms, and asked with a raised eyebrow. "Why are you helping me? After everything you've observed. Why do you stay? Why did you even come to work today?"

Casey shrugged. "I don't know. I guess I knew you would not hurt me. I can sense that you are a good person."

"You are a brave one, Casey. I like that," Kenneth said, a smile suddenly growing on his face. He reached forward, took the bowl, and spoke in between bites. "As you realize, I'm not entirely human. I'm part human, part wolf. What some would call a werewolf."

Suddenly, it made sense. The night before had been a full moon and if the legends were true, that would incite an involuntary transformation where the wolf could not control himself.

"How long have you been this way?" Casey wasn't sure she should ask, but she did anyway. She somehow felt at ease with Kenneth.

"I was born this way. My parents were both werewolves, but some of us are transformed."

Then her thoughts went back to the men from earlier. "Were those guys werewolves, too?"

Kenneth nodded. "Levi is the leader of the pack. A pack that I no longer want to be in."

Casey tilted her head, and her voice softened. "Is that why they did this to you?"

Kenneth didn't have to respond. His silence was her answer. "I want you to promise me you wouldn't engage in any more confrontation with those men."

"Well, technically, they-" Casey started, but Kenneth cut her off.

"Casey, they are dangerous. I want you to promise me you would stay away." Kenneth's nose flared, and he willed her with his eyes. Suddenly she realized why he directed anger towards her and why he abruptly dismissed her before. Kenneth knew what those men were capable of, and he was trying to protect.

"I will," she said, intending to keep this promise.

Chapter 6

When Casey returned home early the next morning, she dropped herself on the couch and fell asleep, cuddled into a ball. The day had been eventful, and she was exhausted, physically and mentally.

Casey spent her entire day lounging around in the apartment, her thoughts straying to Kenneth's bare chest and toned abs. It felt wrong to ogle at him when he was unconscious, but she couldn't help it. Being that close to his half-naked body was torturous.

That evening, Casey dressed with care. Giving her makeup a little more attention than usual. She wore a long-sleeve patterned dress that matched the army green bootie perfectly. Casey didn't want to appear as if she was trying too hard, so she kept her accessories simple, settling for a pearl stud. Her hair was placed into a half-up, half-down style with a few loose strands at the front. The outfit was more elaborate and feminine than what she usually wore for a night shift, but with Kenneth around, her femineity had been awoken.

Kenneth emerged through the main entrance, looking like nothing had happened the previous night after Casey had taken over from Mr. Lessey. He was dressed in jeans and a t-shirt which advertised his toned body. Casey swallowed hard and allowed her feet to give way as her body dropped into the chair at her station.

Kenneth didn't seem to notice the effect he had on her. "Casey," he called, stopping at her desk. "Do you have time after your shift? I would like to take you somewhere."

Casey held back her excitement, shielding her enthusiasm with a composed demeanor. "Sure. I have time. Where do you want to go?"

"It's a surprise," Kenneth said, a one-sided smile framing his lips. "But I guarantee you will like it."

"Ok then," Casey said, pretending to shuffle through papers as Kenneth walked away.

The seconds seemed to drag into each other as Casey waited for the end of her shift. When Mr. Lessey came, her bag was already packed, and she was drumming her fingers against the counter. Kenneth had gone out, instructing her to wait at the front of the building, and this was an instruction she was definitely following.

Kenneth pulled up in a 2015 Toyota Corolla and Casey scampered in without a word. He took her out of the busy city streets to where time seemed to stop, at which point they were the only ones on the road. Casey kept her eyes on the window, mesmerized by the crashing of the waves as it frothed on the white sand. Through the dim light of the receding moon, she was able to appreciate the beauty of the seaside.

Kenneth drove in silence, only stopping when he parked the car on top of a hill overlooking the ocean. "This is my favorite spot," he said, keeping his eyes forward. "I come here sometimes to watch the sunrise."

Casey turned her head in the direction he watched as a flicker of gold highlighted the horizon. The light struck the blue-green waters, giving it the illusion of golden sparkles. "I can see why. This is really beautiful." Casey said nothing after that, taking in the ambiance of their secluded spot.

Long after the sun had fully risen in the sky, Casey spoke again. She didn't want to damper the mood, but she had to know. "Why did you bring me here?" Then she threw up her hands in the air as her question came out unappreciative. "Not that I'm complaining or anything. I just want to know why me. Why share your spot with me?"

Kenneth looked at her, then turned his head away. "I honestly don't know." He breathed out hard. "I just felt a connection to you." He gazed into her eyes then, his jaw twitching. "You are so different from the women I'm used to encountering. I like that."

Different? What did that even mean?

Casey turned away from him as he continued. "You're brave, even in the worst of circumstances. You're smart, beautiful, and funny."

Her cheeks brightened at the sound of his words. "You never give up and you're a good friend, considerate and kind."

It was then her head turned to stare at Kenneth. He only met her three days ago. There was no way he knew all those things about her.

"I was in the club that night," he continued. "The night that pervert attacked you," Kenneth said the words with scorn before his tone became light. "I followed you there."

Casey kept her eyes fixed on him, unsure of how she should interpret his words. "When I saw your applicant picture, it was like I was drawn to you. So I went to your house that day and followed you from there. I'm sorry." Kenneth blew out hard. "I only meant to watch from a distance, but when I saw you in need, I just had to help. I hoped I haven't freaked you out."

Casey shook her head. "Watching your flesh fuse back together didn't scare me off. What makes you think this will?"

The couple held each other's gaze as the space between them minimized. When Kenneth brushed her lips with his, a rush of energy overwhelmed Casey, and she found herself pulling him into her. Her stomach was fluttering and her skin surged with sensitivity.

They clung to each other, Kenneth with his hand wrapped around the small of her back while Casey's was linked behind his neck.

"I feel the same way about you," Casey said when she was finally allowed to breathe. "That sight the other night should have scared me away, but I came back because somehow I knew you were not a threat to me. I knew you wouldn't harm me, and the night before solidified that. I can't stop myself from pulling towards you. I don't want to."

Casey batted her eyelashes, and Kenneth smiled. "Then don't," he said, placing her loose hair behind her ears. "Give into that urge that wants to be with me."

It was Casey who initiated the kiss, pulling Kenneth closer so that her breast pressed against his chest. She moaned into his mouth as her hand went under his shirt, gently stroking his chest.

Kenneth released her to free himself from the material as Casey tugged at the zipper of his jeans. When he was free, she took him in her hand, massaging as his appendage twitched. It didn't take long for him to moisten her hand.

When Casey leaped over the gears to sit on his lap, Kenneth held on to her waist. Then his hand dropped lower and under her dress to caress her thighs. Eventually, his roaming hand slid down to her sensitive area, sliding across the lace of her underwear. Casey held her breath and waited for what was to come.

As Kenneth entered her, her head went backward, and she pushed out her chest. Kenneth's hand went to her rounded mold, and he massaged it as Casey rocked her hips back and forth. Kenneth fit inside her perfectly. It was as if they belonged to each other. He was close to his climax when he felt Casey convulse around his manhood, urging him to follow.

Their orgasm was explosive, wild, and intense, just like their feelings toward each other.

"I never want this feeling to go away," Casey said after she could speak again.

Kenneth smiled and pushed her loose hair behind her ears again. "As long as I'm by your side, it wouldn't."

Chapter 7

The look on Mr. Lessey's face as Kenneth and Casey crossed the lobby to enter Kenneth's apartment together was amusing. The newspaper fell from him with his hand still in the air as he watched them, wide-eyed. Before Kenneth closed the door behind them, Casey noticed him pushing his neck out for a better view.

"I suppose Mr. Lessey is in a state of shock," Kenneth said, turning towards Casey.

Casey had a frown on her face and her eyes were dull. "I supposed coming here was a bad idea."

Kenneth reached out and caressed her shoulders then. "No, it is not. I want you here." Then he placed a kiss on her lips.

The kiss was the start of another intense episode of lovemaking. Casey latched on to Kenneth, pulling him closer as they ravaged each other. Then he unzipped her dress, dropping it to her feet as she kicked the material free.

"Wow," he said, staring at her sultry underwear. It was a purple lace set she had spoiled herself with. "If you wear things like that, I might never make you leave."

Casey smiled and put her hand at her back to unclasp her bra. "What if I wore nothing?" she said, dropping the lacey material to the ground.

"Then you're definitely not leaving." Kenneth pulled her towards him before taking her in his arms and dropping her on the bed. Then he amazed her by tearing this t-shirt and dropping the rags to the side. Casey's eyes widened at the show of masculinity. She was still in awe when Kenneth dropped the rest of his clothing as his manhood sprang free.

He climbed over her then, poking her in the stomach and causing her to giggle.

"Hmm," Kenneth tilted his head. "That is not the sound I want to hear from you."

Casey creased her forehead and pushed up her nose. "What is?"

Kenneth's movement was swift, then. He lowered his body, angling his penis so he slid into Casey's entrance. Casey gasped as she swallowed him. "That is," Kenneth said, displaying a seductive smirk.

Casey grabbed him around the neck and pulled his lips to hers as his thrust caused a tingling sensation in her most sensitive area. With each movement, her sounds became louder, more distinct, until Casey was moaning rather loudly. When she reached her climax, she screamed his name as her body fell backward onto the bed. Kenneth followed her.

"That was amazing," Kenneth said, pulling Casey to him.

She wrapped her feet around him and toyed with the fine hairs on his chest. "Most definitely," she said, with a sparkle in her eye. "But now I'm completely famished."

"Hmm," Kenneth stroked her hair. "Someone made mouthwatering soup for me yesterday. I could warm some up for you?"

Casey pushed herself from the tangled mass of limbs. "Nope. You just lie here and relax. I will take care of it."

Though she intended to make her way to the kitchen, she didn't move at the same time and Kenneth latched on to her arm. "If you don't let me go, we're going to starve to death."

"Then I will die a happy man," he chuckled.

"Not on my watch," Casey said, prying his fingers away, one at a time. When she was free, she sprinted into the kitchen with no clothing. Kenneth followed her about thirty minutes after and by that time Casey had toasted some bread, created a salad, and warmed up the soup. He pulled her in for a kiss before grabbing a bowl.

The couple had almost finished their meal when Casey looked at the mosaic clock and frowned. "It's time for me to take my shift. I suspect Mr. Lessey has already gone."

Kenneth covered her hand with his. "You must be tired. Why don't you go home and rest? I will handle your shift."

He was right. Casey was tired. Not only did she not sleep after her last shift, but she had been doing hard exercise all day.

"Really?" she said, her smile pushing at her cheeks. "You are wonderful."

Kenneth was not beyond being smug. "It's just one of my many traits."

Casey dressed and prepared to leave shortly after that. Her intention was to head home, have a nice long shower, then sleep. Hopefully, until the sun went down again.

She left the apartment first with her eyes partially closed, reminiscing about the day. She hadn't expected to find anyone in the lobby, much less to walk into them.

"I'm so sorry," she said. Backing away from the solid mass, she raised her head to find piercing eyes and a grim expression. It was accompanied by a bald head and fanged teeth.

"Well, look who it is, boys," the leader of the werewolf clan spoke. "I must admit, I was disappointed to not see you behind the desk tonight." He looked past her to where she had emerged from. "But it looks like you got a promotion."

Remembering what she had promised Kenneth, Casey said nothing, kept her head down, and attempted to walk around the man, but he clung to her shoulder. "Don't leave so soon. The fun is just beginning."

"Let me go," she screamed and struggled unsuccessfully in his arms. At the same time, Kenneth burst into the hallway, his eyes raging at the sight that confronted him.

"What are you doing?" he shouted, the veins on his face and neck pronounced. "Let her go."

The bald man smirked, then pushed Casey into the arms of his number one subordinate. "I think you forget your place, Kenneth," he said in a slow, raspy voice. "How dare you tell me what to do?" He made a low sinister growl.

Kenneth lowered his head then but kept his eyes on Casey. "She has nothing to do with this."

The bald man looked back at her. "But she is your weakness." He caressed Casey's cheek. "And having her in my possession means I have control over you."

"You piece of shit," Kenneth said, racing towards the man, but a minion blindsided him and knocked him out.

Chapter 8

Casey screamed as Kenneth fell to the floor, blood flowing from the side of his head. She knew his healing ability was extremely impressive, but what good would it do if he were dead? She struggled free and raced to his side, only to be recaptured. The last thing she remembered before everything went dark was kicking a minion in his most delicate area.

"Casey, can you hear me?" His voice was low, but she knew it well. "Casey, wake up."

Casey groaned and fluttered her eyes open, only to close them again in disbelief.

"Casey, listen to me. I'm going to get you out of here. Do you hear me? I will get you away from all of this."

Casey's head moved slowly as she assessed the situation. She and Kenneth were in an empty room, tied to chairs.

"Where are we?" she asked, still partially dazed.

"We're at the clan's base. Levi plans to make an example of me so no one would dare try to leave the clan again." Kenneth's breath was shallow, and he seemed to be tugging at the bonds on his wrist.

"What's going to happen to us?" Casey's voice was shaky now and some of her words got lost before they reached Kenneth. Her eyes were wide and her lips quivered, giving her the appearance of a child.

"Nothing," Kenneth said firmly, forcing her to look at him. "Because I'm going to get us out of here."

At that time, the door pushed open and the Levi and two of his subordinates entered the room, each sporting a satisfied grin.

"Dammit, Levi." Kenneth roared. "Let us go."

Levi walked slowly towards him. "After I went to all the trouble of summoning the entire clan here. I don't think so."

"We did nothing wrong." Kenneth was still trying to set himself free, but Levi didn't seem concerned.

"You know, in the old days, abandoning your clan was a crime punishable by death." He lowered himself to stare into Kenneth's eyes. "I miss those days. Don't you?" Levi began to pace. "See, you are one of the strongest warrior I have. I had plans to groom you as my second in command. I can't lose you." He looked at Casey, his nose flared. "And definitely not to her."

"I will not fight for you if you harm her." Kenneth was practically screaming.

"I will harm her if you don't," Levi smirked again, this time flashing his elongated canines.

Kenneth remained silent and held his head low. Then suddenly he raised it as if just remembering something. "I challenge you to a duel."

Levi's head whipped around and his voice was hoarse. "What?"

"You heard me." Kenneth kept his voice low and even. "I challenge you, Levi, leader of the clan. If I win, you release us both and never bother us again. And if I lose, I return to the clan and fight for you without resistance."

Levi burst into laughter, his tone amused. "I admit you are a good fighter, Kenneth. But I am the best in this clan. There is no way you can win against me."

"Then you have nothing to worry about," Kenneth blurted.

Levi went quiet for a while, pondering Kenneth's proposition. "Fine then. I look forward to you rejoining the clan."

One of the men released Kenneth then, and he nodded to her before heading for the door. Before Levi left, she told his subordinates. "Bring her. I want her to be there when her boyfriend loses." Then he left.

A minion untied Casey and escorted her to an open room. There was a large crowd around the exterior, but in the middle, Kenneth and Levi, both were preparing themselves mentally for the fight.

Casey didn't know what to expect, but she certainly was not prepared for what she saw. Both men growled and howled as their bodies stressed and morphed out of their human form. Their ears projected first, pointing at the top of their heads before their nose stretched out to the front. Eyes became wide and glowed as their hairs spread across their bodies.

Loud popping sounds were heard as their feet broke and transformed into hind legs while their front ones dropped to the ground. At the end of their transformation, both men stood in the middle of the room as wolves.

Casey squinted her eyes when the black one leaped onto the brown who she knew was Kenneth. He jumped out of the way through, just in time to avoid Levi's attack. Kenneth attacked then, but it backfired.

Casey held her breath as the match went on, squinting at every slash and every bite. It was intense as both wolves were fairly skilled fighters, but it was obvious Levi was the stronger of the two. Kenneth was tenacious though, refusing to give up even as his blood splattered the ground.

When Levi knocked Kenneth off his feet and leaped in the air, Casey closed her eyes and turned her head. She knew Kenneth couldn't take much more.

Seeing nothing but darkness, Casey listened as the crowd gasped, then they cheered loudly, signaling the end of the fight. She took a deep breath and held it, reluctant to open to the light, but when she did, her eyes widened and her heart drummed in her chest. Levi was lying on the ground, his tongue sticking out of his mouth and his stomach rising and dropping.

Kenneth was above him, with his head to the sky, howling in victory.

Chapter 9

Casey held Kenneth around the waist, his hand around her shoulder as she helped him into his room. He was very weak and blood ran down his face and hands, but he was alive. They were both alive and safe, thanks to him.

When she helped him onto the bed, he moaned and closed his eyes. "Tell me what to do?" Casey's eyes were wild as she scanned her lover's body. He was badly wounded, but the cuts had already begun to heal.

"I'm going to need a washcloth," he said. "And time." But Kenneth had a smile on his face.

Casey chuckled, remembering the night before when he had requested the same thing. "Is that all you need?"

Kenneth smirked, and she was happy to see that he was able to lighten the situation. It meant that he was not critical. "The other thing I already have."

Though she knew his answer would be a strange remark, Casey asked, "What is that?"

Kenneth held her hand and pulled her down to him. "You."

Casey gave him a friendly smack on the shoulder and pushed herself standing again. "Well, if you have this much energy, you can make your way to the bathroom. Go have a bathe," she instructed. "The blood is bothering me."

Then there was that smirk again. "Only if you join me."

"I am not the filthy one." Casey tilted her head and pushed up her eyebrows.

She should have backed away before Kenneth took his hand and rubbed it all over her. "Now you are."

She eyed him crossly, but there was a playful smile on her lips. "Fine," she told him, pulling him from the bed. "We can both take a bath."

Kenneth's expression was one of being proud. He engulfed Casey in his arms and led her to the bathroom.

The water was warm and refreshingly sprayed the couple. Kenneth wrapped Casey in his arms and placed a kiss on his forehead. "I know I haven't been in your life long, but I don't know what I would do without you, Casey. You give my life meaning." Then he looked into her eyes, his words soft and filled with emotions. "I love you."

Casey's eyes were bright. It might have been the spray from the shower, but they were filled with moisture too. She smiled wildly and looped her hand around Kenneth's neck. "My life was definitely less eventful without you. But it was also more lonely." She pressed her body against him, her wet breast sliding on his toned chest, sending sensations throughout her body. "I love you too."

Their lips met under the stream of water as their kiss intensified. Then Kenneth turned her around and pinned her against the wall so that he faced her back. Casey's hand took purchase on the wall as her lover bent her over and passed his hand on her ass before smacking it. Casey felt his penis on her entrance then, hard and ready to enter her, but it didn't.

She groaned. "What are you waiting for?"

"I want to hear you say it. Tell me you want me," Kenneth passed his hand on her ass again before settling it on her waist.

"I want you, Kenneth. I want you much. I can't take it anymore. Take me now." Casey had barely finished her sentence when she felt his intrusion. His cock was warm and welcomed as it slid along the walls of her vagina. She moaned and pushed herself backward, sending more of him inside her. She only stopped at the shaft.

"So impatient," Kenneth said with a chuckle but began to incite her with a forceful thrust. Casey moaned with each one, clinging to the wet surface of the tiles. She pushed her ass backward every time Kenneth eased away from her, always needing to feel him inside. Her intensity that built throughout the entire act was breathtakingly passionate. When the surge finally took over her body, she fisted her hands and released a passionate moan. Kenneth wasn't finished, though. He went a few more rounds before finally releasing himself.

When they were finished, the two made their way to the bedroom. Kenneth gave Casey a t-shirt that fit her like a dress so she could wash the outfit she had. They were about to enter the kitchen to prepare a meal together when they heard a commotion in the lobby.

"Stay here," Kenneth said with his eyes narrowed and forehead creased. "I'm going to check it out."

Casey nodded, but as soon as he moved away, she took a step behind him. Kenneth walked out into the hallway and to the lobby, then suddenly stopped. Casey bumped into his back and when she peered her head to the side to see beyond his frame, her eyes widened. The lobby was filled with well-built men, each one sexier than the next, but none matching Kenneth. She recognized some of them from the fight. Two were Levi's minions.

"You've proved yourself the strongest in our clan and you were always a good leader," a blond man with blue eyes came forward. "We come to you today requesting that we join your clan. We all want to follow you."

Casey came to his side then, and his fingers laced through hers with a smile. Then he turned to the men who made the lobby seem smaller than it actually was. "Together, we would become the strongest clan."

The men erupted in cheers and hoots.

THE END

The Wild Side Fantasy

Description

Jane is not a plain lady. She was a student at the Art Institute of Chicago. She had fire engine red hair, but, as an art student, she referred to her hair color as "magenta." Jane enjoyed this endless assortment of 'normal' men. She loved to stand in contrast to them.

They were so different from the boys at her school. The boys at her school clung so desperately to their counterculture looks, their alternative tastes. They slouched at parties holding their drinks as if they'd practiced their facial expressions in the mirror for hours. Jane had gone to bed (or to the bathroom or to the lawn) with many of these boys and although many of these boys could talk the talk, they couldn't fuck the fuck. They were boring lays to her.

Much of this sex was some hurried version of the missionary position and there was some licking involved and that was about it. Jane fantasized about giving a wholesome, real, delicious man a chance to explore her wild side. And then she met with Rusty, an all-American man in his early thirties.

Chapter 1

Jane was not plain. She was a student at the Art Institute of Chicago. She had fire engine red hair, but, as an art student, she referred to her hair color as "magenta." She wore her hair in an old fashioned bob with bangs and people often mistook it for a wig. She had to touch up her dark brown roots every three weeks, as her hair grew rather quickly, by bleaching it first and then adding the "magenta" rinse. It was the purest of reds, she'd say.

She had her septum pierced, her nipples pierced, her navel pierced. Jane had a sprinkling of tattoos, in various places, both publicly visible and not. To the casual onlooker they appeared to all have been obtained on a whim, as there was no unifying theme, no single solitary work of art, but to Jane they were all purposeful and had profound meaning. She was short in stature and wore tight fitting clothes to show off her muscular physique. She lifted weights five times a week.

Jane worked at the flower shop two blocks down from the Art Institute. She enjoyed putting together flower bouquets on the spot for customers. They'd come in asking for something feminine, or something with jewel tones, or something that looked like wildflowers and she'd be able to put together an assortment within their price range. She enjoyed grouping the colors together, making sure there was a variety of forms, both rounded flowers and tall skinny flowers. She took pride in her little job.

She also took pride in being far more intelligent than she appeared. In school she wrote both essays and longer papers about things like the sexuality of Northern Renaissance still life painting, about the mixed political motivations behind criticisms of photographs by Andres Serrano and Robert Mapplethorpe, about the movement of Russian Avant Garde to Stalinist Socialist Realism. However, her major was in ceramics. And although her professor considered her a savant at the potter's wheel, she preferred hand building, coil building human like sculptures. She had strong hands.

Jane's boss at the flower shop often called upon her to use her writing skills to write letters for the shop, letters to brides to let them know of their wedding estimates, retorts to nasty letters from angry customers who were upset about this detail or that.

At the flower shop there were regular customers and those who just dropped in once or twice. But there were other 'regulars' at the flower shop. There were the designers, who designed the flower arrangements, the drivers (the weekend drivers and the weekday drivers), the UPS man, the mail man, the flower shipment delivery man, the gift item delivery man (who delivered things like baskets, vases, gift cards and the like). Most of the customers to walk through the door of the flower shop were men.

Jane enjoyed this endless assortment of 'normal' men. She loved to stand in contrast to them. They were so different from the boys at school. The boys at school clung so desperately to their counterculture looks, their alternative tastes. They slouched at parties holding their drinks as if they'd practiced their facial expressions in the mirror for hours.

Jane had gone to bed with (or to the bathroom with, or to the lawn with) many of these boys and although many of these boys could talk the talk, they couldn't fuck the fuck. They were boring lays. Much of this sex was some hurried version of the missionary position and there was some licking involved and that was about it. But these men at the flower shop were wholesome, real, seemingly delicious. Jane fantasized about having a chance to sink her teeth into one of them, blow their minds with her wild side.

"Maybe the UPS man," Jane fantasized. Jane was confident. She liked that the UPS man's socks matched his uniform. She liked the way he said, "Sign here," with authority. She liked the way he hopped into his truck and drove off, as if into the sunset.

But this isn't the story of Jane and the UPS man. This is the story of how Jane met Rusty. Rusty was an all-American man in his early thirties. He was a firefighter and a new regular customer at the flower shop. Rusty was huge. Not only was he tall and very well built, but he sometimes came into the flower shop still in his firefighter gear, which seemed to make his feet larger, his legs longer, his shoulders broader. At first he came in once a week, on Fridays, getting flowers for his girlfriend.

He'd ask for something pink, or something orange, something simple, tulips, when he asked for lisianthus, a particularly delicate flower, Jane recommended special greens for him, when he asked for lavender roses Jane recommended a dried pink filler because baby's breath was too predictable, too obvious for that particular shade of rose. Jane took good care of Rusty. She was kind to him.

Rusty began coming to the shop on Wednesdays too. He began wooing his current girlfriend more aggressively. Rusty had a secret, a reason for this aggressive wooing. Rusty wasn't really your typical all-American boy next door all grown up.

Rusty was a sadomasochist. He had been that way as long as he could remember.

Whenever he saw comic books as a kid, and they showed damsels in distress and other boys were overwhelmed with the desire to rescue them, he was overwhelmed with how beautiful they looked right then and there. Every time he met a girl, every time he revealed his secret to her, she went running. Every girl. He was afraid his current girl would do the same.

He'd tried hiding his secret from girls, but that never lasted. A bite would always land on a nipple, a slap would always land on a cheek and the slap was often returned. He'd spent many a shameful and hurried evening purchasing pornography to relieve his tension. And although Rusty was a sadomasochist, he was still wholesome. He wasn't going to clubs and bars. He wanted to meet a "nice girl," not some bar slut.

His current girlfriend, Melissa, was a nice girl; she was a nurse's aid. He wanted to get it right with her. He wanted her to understand him, his desires, accept him. Thus, the wooing. But because Rusty had never gone to bars, had never tried online sex, had never become part of 'the community' Rusty had no clue as to how to verbalize his desires to another human being.

And he had no idea how to express himself sexually. He knew he liked the sight of a woman tied up, he knew he was overwhelmed with urges to bite and slap, he sometimes knew what he liked when he watched pornography, but all in all Rusty was a confused and conflicted man. He was at a complete loss because of his desire to remain "decent," and because of this desire he was doomed to fail with women again and again.

Jane picked up on the tension building in Rusty. Every time he came into the flower shop he was more and more nervous. Rusty felt as if he wasn't going to be able to hold back much longer. Something was bound to happen soon. One day, when he had picked out a dozen red roses filled with eucalyptus leaves Jane took in the sight of this massive, bulky, save-the-day type man wringing his hands. She felt bad for Rusty and wanted to ease his tension.

"You know if I didn't know any better I'd say you were about to pop the question or something. You're all nervous. You're buying more and more flowers. They're more and more expensive." Jane was blunt.

"Me? No. No. Not that. Just a big night. Hope she likes me," he stuttered.

Rusty was obviously a taken man and Jane was obviously not his type so it felt safe for Jane to speak her mind. "What do you have to worry about? You're totally hot, you're a firefighter, you're, like, a knight in shining armor. You'll be fine," said Jane, waving one hand in the air casually as she rung up his order.

"A knight in shining armor. That's funny," he responded and took his flowers and left. Jane didn't see him again for three weeks. and often wondered about her wholesome tortured knight.

Chapter 2

Jane woke up in her dormitory to the sound of a fire alarm. Again. It was likely to be another hippy burning too much incense. She stepped into her bunny slippers and wandered outside noting the time on her way out. It was 2:34. And it was cold. She had a morning class the next day. On her way out her shoulder bumped into Rusty's elbow as he was on his way in. They both turned around to look at each other.

Jane had seen Rusty in some of his gear before but not all of it. He looked massive. Jane looked tiny and compact. She was just over five feet tall and she had to put knots in her camisole straps to keep them from being too long and exposing her small breasts. As it was, they were still in danger of being exposed. The camisole was made of thin cotton and Rusty's eyes quizzically rested upon Jane's nipples.

"What? It's cold," Jane laughed nonchalantly, innocently. Guys have stared at her nipples like that before. She knew exactly why he was staring at her nipples. Rusty wasn't thinking about the hardness of Jane's nipples. He was thinking about the obvious piercings through them. Rusty was wondering why she had done that. Jane turned and walked away. She went to the fire truck and waited for Rusty there, her bunny slippered ankles crossed, her arms folded across her chest. Rusty finally came back out from the dormitory, mask under his arm.

"You can go back inside," he said.

"Are you at least gonna tell me who I can be pissed at?" Jane asked.

"You know I can't tell you that," Rusty replied.

"C'mon."

"I can tell you someone lit a candle and then put it inside a wooden bookshelf," said Rusty, rolling his eyes and smiling.

"Oh my God! The admissions committee selects us from far and wide. All over the world. We're supposed to be smart! This is ridiculous!" laughed Jane. It was pretty ridiculous.

Jane and Rusty shared a laugh at an anonymous student's expense. During their laugh Rusty stole glances of Jane, her tattoos, her pajama pants rolled down at the waistband revealing her abdominal muscles and part of a spider tattoo, those nipples, eyes laughing from behind smeared, slept-on eyeliner.

"I gotta go to bed. I have a morning class," said Jane turning around on her toes hesitantly and walking away, her firm, muscular buttocks protruding with each step.

"Jane!" What are you doing? She's in college. She's on campus. You're working! She did say you were hot... Jane turned back around, her finger in her mouth, her head down but eyes peering up with an over the top charm only an of-age college girl could pull off. "Do you want to get coffee sometime?"

Jane remarked, "That would be great. Yeah. I'll drop by the firehouse on my way to the flower shop Tuesday."

"Tuesday." Rusty smiled genuinely. Jane made him feel just plain good. She wasn't like the other girls, then again she wasn't what he was really looking for either.

Tuesday morning Jane got up at 10:30. She didn't have any classes on Tuesdays, she didn't have work on Tuesdays until 5pm. The flower shop was open until 8pm. Tuesdays were mostly free. Jane went to the gym, ran on the treadmill, lifted weights, came back to her dorm room and showered.

She washed and carefully set her hair. She opened her closet and contemplated what to wear. What does one wear? Out with a firefighter? Jane was excited to go out with a decent, normal guy. This was just what she had been fantasizing about. But why did he like her? Why had he invited her out?

She remembered the way he'd eyed her during their conversation, her tattoos, her piercings. She briefly considered "dressing down," dressing like more of a normal person, maybe a flower print dress, but then decided Rusty must like her for her. So she put on her usual skinny jeans, her favorite pair actually, with a white belt, converse, tight tee-shirt, and blue scarf knotted at her neck. She tossed her bag over her shoulder and walked to the firehouse.

When she got to the firehouse the garage door was open. She went through it and through the door at the opposite end of it and up a set of stairs. The stairs led to a kitchen where she found Rusty and two other firefighters cleaning up after an early lunch.

"Hi. Rusty," said Jane curtly, waving her hand in the air quickly, nervously. The sight of those other firefighters made her feel anxious, as if they had been caught in the raptures of their unacceptable love. But there was no love. Jane was just the girl on the other side of the counter for Rusty. And there was nothing unacceptable, Jane was twenty-one, of age to handle a relationship with a man in his early thirties. They just looked a little different.

"You must be Jane," said one of the firefighters, extending his hand. Jane shook it. "I'm Bob." Bob walked away.

"Hi. I'm Drew." Jane shook Drew's hand and Drew walked away.

"They sure left in a hurry," giggled Jane. "You been talkin' about me?"

"Maybe a little bit. Gotta warn the guys when a girl covered in tattoos is comin' to the firehouse."

"I know!" Jane said. "I don't wanna freak them out! So where do you wanna go? I see you have some coffee right there." She was hoping to stay at the firehouse, hoping things would move along quickly.

"Ah that stuff? That stuff is awful! You don't want that! I know a great place around the block."

"Skippy's? By the bookstore?" asked Jane. "I love that place!"

Rusty extended his arm to Jane, chivalrously and overly dramatically, having to bend his knees so she could reach him. He was well over six feet tall. Jane enthusiastically took his arm and they walked together to the coffee shop, closely, feeling each other's strides, feeling each other's sides pressed up against one another. They shared a silence with each other as they walked around the block to Skippy's.

Once seated, Jane had to ask, "So why are you a firefighter? What makes you want to run into burning buildings for a living? Why not be an accountant? That's safe."

"Well..."

Wow. Jane had gone to the heart of it right from the beginning. He could barely admit this to himself but he got off on seeing women tied up and tortured, so rescuing people seemed to make up for it, being a firefighter he really could be a knight in shining armor, at least momentarily, even though really he wanted things that seemed far more dark and evil. "My dad was a firefighter. So I thought I'd follow in his footsteps." Rusty grimaced.

Jane could see there was something else there and she knew she would get to the bottom of it.

Rusty could wait no longer. It was his turn to ask, "So why all the piercings. Why all the tattoos? Didn't all that stuff hurt?"

Jane exhaled. "I have a unique relationship with pain," she said, licking cappuccino foam off her thumb. Rusty raised an eyebrow. "Some things that are considered painful, I find enjoyable. Like my tattoos, some people like to go to their 'happy place' when they're getting tattooed, but not me. I like to really feel the pain. Really be there for it. And I consider all of these things adornments to my body. I take good care of my body, I work out, I'm just adorning it."

Rusty thought she had a nice body.

Rusty sipped his coffee. Jane enjoyed hers. They shared another silence having gotten out of the way what was bugging them each the most.

"So, you go to the Art Institute. That's supposed to be a good school. What kind of art do you do?" asked Rusty.

"I do ceramics. Hand building. Both figural and abstract," Jane answered, nodding. Rusty had no idea what she was talking about.

"I'd like to see it some time."

"You can come see it right now." Jane felt suddenly shy and withdrew. "If you have time."

"No. That'd be great. I'd love to see your... work," said Rusty. He was intrigued by this woman who had a 'unique relationship with pain.' He wanted more insight into her. This woman. This girl. She seemed to like him. He wondered what he was doing with her. But he paid for the coffee and offered her his arm again, she accepted it again, and they walked the three blocks to the Art Institute.

When they reached the ceramics studio no one was there. The door was locked and Jane rummaged in her bag for the key. Rusty stuffed his hands in his pockets and looked around. Jane opened the sticky door by ramming her shoulder into it. The studio was divided into three sections. On the right were several kilns and the left section was divided in the middle by floor to ceiling shelves filled with sculptures and bowls and cups. Behind the shelves were several potter's wheels, in front of them, several working tables.

"Well. This is my studio," Jane remarked, arms extended. "My sculptures are this way... Let me get the light."

She reached for the light switches. Rusty reached for her hand on the light switch, ran his fingers along her arm, and paused at her shoulder. She looked up at him invitingly. God. Finally. She bit her own lip and turned down her perfectly lined eyes.

She wasn't a good girl, she wasn't what Rusty was looking for. Rusty had nothing to lose with Jane. He decided he'd give in to his desires. Just a little bit. He pushed her shoulder up against the wall with his hand. He grabbed the back of her head with the other and slouched down low enough that he could kiss her deeply, harshly, biting her lip, her tongue, his knees bent around her legs, his arms pressing her, enveloping her, the wall pressing on her back.

She was caged by his enormous body. Then he stopped, stepped back, wiped his mouth and waited for her response, half waiting to get slapped on the face again, half hoping to get kissed again.

"Not here," she said and she grabbed him by the wrist and led him to her dormitory. Menacing fantasies welled up in Rusty's mind during that walk. As did in Jane's. To her, here was her "normal" guy. She hadn't picked up on the biting, the pushing. To her, here was her chance to blow someone away with her freaky side. She unlocked her door and they both stepped in. Rusty looked around as he closed the door behind him.

Chapter 3

The ceiling was lined with a row of shelving filled with undulating pots and sculptures. There was a mirror with a dresser in front of it that had the remains of Jane's primping ritual atop it: rollers, scattered makeup, a fine toothed comb. Jane took a few steps backwards towards her bed. Rusty walked towards her. She pushed him. She was used to being the stronger one in the bedroom. All those skinny art school boys.

"So, do you have a roommate I should be worried about coming through the door?" asked Rusty. He was feeling confident now. He pushed her back. He was stronger than her.

"No. I'm a senior." Jane fell on the bed and laughed.

This laughter provoked Rusty. He was revealing himself to her faster than he had to any other woman and she was laughing at him? Or was she just having a good time? He pushed her down onto the bed and kissed her deeply, his legs kneeling around her legs, his arms bent around her shoulders. He used his right hand to undo her belt.

Crap. Jane had worn the tightest pair of jeans she owned precisely because they looked fantastic on her ass, NOT because they came off with ease in the bedroom. She had to do a special little dance just to get them on. Getting them off was a whole 'nother special little dance. Maybe she should've gone for the flower print dress. She hadn't expected things to happen so quickly with Rusty. Rusty was able to pull the belt from her pants with one swift gesture and Jane had renewed faith that, between the two of them, they could get her pants off with minimal clumsiness.

Rusty kneeled up over her. The way he looked at her, his eyes seemed chaotic, he seemed hungry. He pulled off each shoe without untying it and threw it across the room. He unbuttoned and unzipped her pants and pulled them off with two tugs, first to the knees, then clean off. She was impressed.

She was wearing a blue g-string with orange trim. It seemed to match the scarf she was still wearing.

"Complimentary colors," she said, running her fingers along the trim and giggling. Rusty was so turned on by this incessant giggling and laughing because it provoked him, it inflamed him because it at once made him angry at the possibility she was laughing at him, and put him at ease that this whole thing was no big deal. Both emotions made him want to explore his more sinister side.

He savagely pulled up her shirt revealing her pierced nipples and navel and a number of tattoos but he left the shirt on, he left her scarf on and suddenly flipped her over. Jane felt shocked by his sheer strength, his strength over her. She wanted to rock some generic man's world but it was becoming clear it was her world that was about to be rocked.

She lay flat for just a moment and was lifted her by her belly with his arm into the kneeling position. He used both hands to slowly pull her g-string down, following the strings with his lips. Jane felt his tongue run down her ass, down her pussy. His tongue lingered there, savoring the taste of her, exploring her crevices irregularly, pausing here for a moment, pausing there for longer, licking the entirety of her slit several times to ensure he would taste the moisture that was building up inside of her.

He massaged her firm, unyielding ass as he did this, running his hands around each mound, squeezing it, pulling it open, pulling Jane open so he could see her, taste her. He left her panties around her knees. Jane felt a slight tinge of shame with them there. She wanted to keep them there. She wanted to curl up and take comfort in this bigger, older man's power over her.

All at once Rusty's lips and tongue and hands disappeared. Jane knelt below him, waiting to see what was next, immobile, blinking. Rusty knelt above her, looking down at her, her ass in the air, her shirt pulled up, a scarf around her neck. I have a unique relationship with pain. Rusty landed one single, solitary and very hard smack on Jane's rear end. Jane felt it on her skin, then in the muscles of her butt, then in her gut, then she felt it pulsate in her lungs. Then she felt a brief, "Ah-ah," come out of her mouth. She turned around to look at Rusty in surprise. Rusty's hand was still in the air, his mouth was open and he was looking at his hand. He looked at Jane.

"I'm sorry?" he said, an erection bulging through his tight jeans.

"Don't be. Do it again."

"I... I don't think so. I don't think I should," Rusty stammered, trying to ignore the erection that was now becoming quite evident through his jeans.

"Don't be silly," Jane laughed. "That was great." Jane arched her back, raising her ass higher in the air. She'd never been spanked before, but it was exhilarating. She was game to try anything new.

That laugh, Rusty shook it off. "No. Men aren't supposed to beat women." Rusty subconsciously stroked at his throbbing cock through his pants.

"You're not beating me, you're spanking me. There's a difference," she said, matter-of-factly. Jane slowly waved her ass from side to side, chin resting in her palms, waiting.

"Are you sure you want this?" Rusty asked.

"Sure. Look, if I get too freaked out or it hurts too much I'll just say alstromeria," Jane was now facing Rusty and was trying to comfort him. His erection was persistent despite the inner turmoil he was experiencing. Jane couldn't ignore it. She unzipped his pants and pulled it out. She cupped his testicles in one hand and stroked his cock with the other in a twisting motion.

Rusty exhaled and dropped back his head. Jane would lift her hand, twisting it with the skin of his cock and then twist it back on the way down, at the same time pulling at his balls. She leaned down and swallowed the head of his penis. It was enough to fill her entire mouth. She suckled on it, moving it in and out of her mouth, swirling her tongue around its head, all the while moving her hand up and down in this twisting motion, squeezing him with her strong ceramicist hands harder and harder, and pulling at his balls.

"Okay," Rusty sighed. Jane turned back around and arched her back even more this time and Rusty smacked her again and Jane felt the same sense of exhilaration, but this time, Rusty felt it too. For the first time in his life he felt it willingly. He smacked her again and again, harder and harder until Jane's ass was nearly purple and she belted out, "Oh my God!"

"Are you okay?" he asked, flipping her over so she was sitting down, facing him, knees up. Jane's body was languid, her lined eyes blinked lazily, she had drooled on the bed.

"I'm fine," said Jane, out of breath, a strand of magenta hair caught between her lips. She gave him two thumbs up and a smile and fell back onto her elbows. She put her feet on his chest and ran her right toes, nails painted green, down to his now completely engorged member. "How are you?"

Rusty took off his belt with the same single motion he used to remove Jane's and took off his pants. His legs were muscular. He kneeled at the foot of the bed and bit Jane's toes, he bit at her thighs, he bit her pussy, he bit the outline of her abdominal muscles, he bit her nipples, he bit her lips, he showered her in caresses of painful kisses to which Jane occasionally responded with an, "Ah."

Once he reached her lips Jane bit him back. He bit her harder, tugging at her lower lip as though he were going to pull it off and grabbed her scarf at the knot stopping to make sure this was okay. Jane nodded. He pulled the knot down to the mattress choking Jane and he pressed himself into her. Jane let out a gurgled moan.

He thrust himself into her slowly at first, like he always had with women, breathing into her ear. But the sound of her altered, obstructed breath provoked him like nothing ever had. He stood up on his hands and began pumping himself into her as hard as he could, rhythmically, in a somewhat rounded motion, his right hand still pressing down at the knot of Jane's scarf.

He pushed himself into her so hard that the whole lower half of her body was raised up to Rusty, who was kneeling on the bed. Jane was hypnotized by this rhythm, this fucking, she touched her body, she pulled at her nipples, her clit, trying to recreate the special kisses he had bestowed upon her.

She tried to kiss Rusty but Rusty just pushed her down by her forehead. His cock was long and thick, the head of which was even thicker and with every motion Jane could feel its contour in her. He pushed her inner labia in and out, her juices mixed with his until finally there was nothing but a suction sound and the occasional sound of the two mouths exhaling.

Rusty rolled her over on top of him and held her body up over him by her neck. He pressed her legs open with his and thrust into her with cadence and momentum. This position seemed to particularly excite Jane as Rusty rubbed his body against her clit with every forceful push. She let out a hindered exhalation or moan or whimper with each drive into her body.

Rusty, still holding her by the neck threw her onto the floor. He jumped onto her. He kneeled above her and looked at her like an animal might look at prey. His cock was wet from her juices now and he placed her feet onto his chest. He placed his fingers onto her anus. She looked at him and relaxed. He slowly slid his soaking wet cock into her ass, millimeters at a time, watching her face, taking care not to hurt her. But once he was in all the way he began moving in and out, faster and faster.

She was so tight, she was such a tiny girl. Jane braced herself with one hand on the bottom of the dresser and one hand on the bottom of her desk. She felt carpet burn forming on her lower back, a point of pride.

He was so big, her mouth was open out of sheer shock that she, such a petite woman, was even able to take in such a huge man. Rusty began driving himself into her harder and harder, more and more rhythmically until finally Rusty couldn't manage the rhythm anymore, he pulled out and came all over Jane's perfectly formed abdominals.

"Oh my God. I'm sorry. Are you okay? I'm so sorry. Are you okay?" Rusty was flustered, and ashamed.

"It's cool! I'm all right. Here. Let me get a towel for you... us." Jane giggled, out of breath, flustered too. She got a towel and they silently wiped off the evidence of Rusty's deepest, darkest secret. Jane pushed Rusty gently back into the bed and curled up into his big arms. He had shown her something new in so many ways, he wasn't like the art school boys in so many ways. He was just a regular guy on the outside, but in the bedroom he was a wild animal, he had shown her a side of herself she couldn't believe she hadn't explored before.

She was grateful to Rusty as she lay there, running her fingers through the chest hairs that stuck out from his tee-shirt. They both lay there in their tee-shirts, but Rusty's mind was in a different place. He felt shame in what he had done to Jane. He felt it was wrong, wrong to treat a woman, a girl like that. He felt shame in what he had done, but at the same time Jane felt so good in his arms, so tiny, she made him feel big, masculine.

Jane popped her head up. "What time is it?"

"Four twenty," Rusty said, looking at his watch.

"I gotta get ready for work!" Jane said, hopping out of bed, kissing Rusty on the lips, pausing to smile at him. Rusty looked away. "Hey," she said, grabbing his face in her hands, "This was fantastic. I mean it." Jane got out of bed and walked over to the dresser; she picked up the fine toothed comb and carefully ran it through her disheveled hair, finishing it off with her hand.

"Do you think we could have coffee again?" Jane asked lightheartedly as she did her tight skinny jeans dance.

"Yeah, sure. Drop by the firehouse," said Rusty, laughing a little at Jane's jeans dance, feeling a little optimistic because he was still feeling the warmth of Jane's body in his arms. She felt so right there. He put on his pants and his belt and discretely left the building.

Jane dropped by the firehouse the very next day. She wanted to know more about her wholesome tortured knight. Where did he go to school? Who did he go to the prom with? Did he always want to be a firefighter? What was his favorite color? What was his favorite food? When she walked up the stairs and into the kitchen Rusty was sitting at the table eating a bowl of chili and Bob was washing dishes.

"Hi Rusty. Hi Bob," Jane said.

"Heyyy, Jane! Didn't think we'd see ya back so soon! How are ya?" asked Bob shaking Jane's hand overly enthusiastically.

"I'm good. Thanks! How are you?"

"Good," said Bob, exhaling and rubbing his slight belly. "Your friend here is an excellent chef. You should try some of his chili."

"Really?" said Jane inquisitively. "I had no idea." She faked a pouty glare at Rusty who continued to look down into his bowl. Bob noted the tension and excused himself. Jane spun around and plopped herself in Rusty's lap, wrapping her arms around his neck and crossing her legs. Rusty stiffened but he couldn't ignore her there. She ran her finger along his profile, down his forehead, his nose, and along his lips. This seemed to weaken this stubbornly distant man momentarily.

"Rusty? What's the matter?" She pouted some more.

"I just..." Rusty searched for the courage. "I just don't think what we did was right. I don't think what was between us was right."

"But Rusty, don't be silly," Jane ran her fingers through his hair and looked carefully at each feature on his face, his well defined lips, his full eyebrows, she looked back and forth between each speckled blue eye. "What we shared was wonderful. For you and for me. We can be ourselves around each other. It doesn't matter how different we look."

"No. A man shouldn't do that to a woman. I'm sorry Jane. You bring out bad things in me, things I need to overcome." Rusty scooted his chair out and stood up and, in doing so, pushed Jane off his lap. Jane stumbled. He went to the sink and washed his bowl, turning his back to Jane. "I think you should go."

"Rusty are you sure? Have you thought about this? Don't you remember –"

"Go!" Rusty cut her off. He didn't want anyone hearing any of the details of their encounter. He felt nothing but shame, he remembered nothing but wickedness. He'd already forgotten the sense of freedom he felt the second time he spanked her and allowed himself to enjoy it, he'd already forgotten the sense of power he felt when he was choking her and fucking her harder than he'd fucked anyone before, he'd forgotten how masculine he felt holding her tiny body in his arms.

Jane scoffed. She dropped her hands to her thighs. She turned around and walked out of the firehouse. For the next six months Jane and Rusty searched for each other in other people.

Rusty searched for Jane in "good girls." He sought out diminutive women, women who laughed a lot, women who loved art. But his relationships always failed; Rusty never could gain control over his passions and these good girls always left him.

Jane searched for Rusty in her circle of art school friends. She looked for well built muscular boys, she desperately searched for someone to spank her, to bite her, she positioned boys' arms to mimic the way she walked arm in arm with Rusty, but none of it felt right. No one fit the bill. It never worked when she had to tell them to spank her, tell them to grab her by the arm. Rusty never returned to the flower shop. Neither of them ever returned to Skippy's.

Whenever Jane walked past the firehouse on the way to the flower shop she quickened her pace, for fear of running into Rusty, seeing him washing the fire truck or sliding down the pole on the way to a call. Whenever Jane walked past the firehouse on the way to the flower shop the scab of that moment in the kitchen was torn off and she felt the pain of being thrown out all over again. Jane started going the long way, around the block to avoid the firehouse altogether. She wished things had gone differently, but as it was, she never wanted to see Rusty again.

Chapter 4

Jane was on a date with Thomas. She had been on lots of dates with lots of guys since Rusty but Thomas seemed different. He had read all the right books. He liked all the right art. He said all the right things about Jane's sculptures. He wasn't a sadomasochist per se, but was at least willing to try things in the bedroom under Jane's guidance. He wore black rimmed glasses and messy blond hair.

He was the same age as Jane. He was skinny, but Jane was willing to forgive this flaw. It was Wednesday night and he and Jane were hanging out in her bedroom after a poetry reading on campus.

"I thought she was amazing!" said Jane.

"She was alright," Thomas put in. "I don't know. Maybe I'm just not into Black Lesbian Poetry. Maybe I just can't relate."

"I'm not black. I'm not a lesbian. I can relate. I can appreciate it," Jane capitulated.

Thomas took off Jane's jacket and placed it on her chair. Then he took off her tee-shirt. She was wearing a turquoise bra and removed. He let her do her skinny jeans dance herself. He did his own skinny jeans dance out of his black skinny jeans.

They performed this ritual almost robotically, as though they had performed it a thousand times. They climbed onto the bed, Jane first, crawling, Thomas sighing because he knew what this crawling meant.

Jane stopped mid-crawl and looked back at Thomas. Thomas knew what to do. He slapped her ass. Jane felt a slight sense of relief from her tension. She was glad to have had found someone who was willing to humor her, willing to be somewhat adventurous in the bedroom. Maybe, she'd hoped, maybe he'd get a paddle. Thomas was willing to spank and bite, but that was it. Jane was beginning to believe that was enough for her.

Jane was becoming genuinely happy with Thomas. He wasn't tortured. He never kicked her out. And he was more like her. He had tattoos. He dressed like her.

But their pseudo role play was interrupted. There was a knock at the door.

"Just a minute!"

Jane quickly threw on a tee-shirt that had probably been lying on the floor for a week and answered it.

Rusty was on an early weekday date with Carol, a fifth grade school teacher. She had shoulder length blond hair that fell in locks upon her shoulders. She was wearing a red and pink floral printed dress with short sleeves and a red, shiny belt. It was their fifth date. Rusty walked her home around seven thirty and she invited him in.

"Do you want a cup of coffee?" asked Carol from her kitchen as Rusty paced nervously in her living room.

"No. I'll take another beer if you have one."

"Aren't you sure you've had enough?" Carol warned.

"I weigh 274 pounds, I'm six foot four. Carol, I can handle a few beers," said Rusty, condescendingly. The truth was, Rusty was a little drunk already. He was nervous. He knew it was about that time, as it was with all his relationships, that his true nature would be revealed and Carol's commitment to him would be tested. Carol was so nice, so pretty.

"Well okay," said Carol, popping open another beer for Rusty and handing it to him. They stood across from one another, looking into each other's eyes in the hallway in between Carol's kitchen and her living room/dining room space. Rusty chugged his beer.

"If I didn't know any better, I'd think you had something to be nervous about," said Carol, tapping him on the chest and walking over to the couch, hesitating before she sat down. "Do you have something to be nervous about?"

Rusty came over to the couch and sat down. He ran his fingers through her hair and grabbed the back of her neck. He kissed her deeply, trying to express his powerful emotions to her. He pressed her head into his with one hand, massaging her shoulder forcefully with the other. Carol pulled away from his advances.

"You're so forward tonight," she said.

"I guess I'm just really feeling strongly. You look so incredibly beautiful."

Carol blushed. She was dressed in a very old fashioned dress, one that one of those damsels in distress might have worn. She would have looked stunning tied to a pair of railroad tracks, her red lips contorted into a scowl, her hands fully extended trying to break free from the rope, her red pumped feet kicking in vain.

Rusty was getting sidetracked but he couldn't get that image of Carol out of his head. Those pumps, that dress with the thin red belt, those lips. He had to possess her like that. He grabbed her by the shoulders and kissed her once on the lips, decisively. She laughed. Rusty immediately remembered the way Jane had laughed, the way her laugher at once incited him and indicated to him everything was okay, that he was okay.

Rusty took this laugh as the go-ahead. He pushed Carol down onto the couch and lay on top of her. He smothered her with his weight. He ran his fingers through her hair again, this time pulling it a little. He pressed on her shoulders with his hand. He squeezed her breast hard, pulling at her nipple.

"Stop Rusty. You're hurting me! What are you doing?" Carol exclaimed. "This isn't the gentle Rusty I know." She pushed him off of her.

"Yeah well..." Here it was again. The end of another relationship. Rusty slurred his speech. "The gentle Rusty you know isn't so gentle deep down."

He was drunk. Now he'd said something that surprised even him. He had admitted to himself, out loud, and to Carol, that he was not a gentle man when it came to women. And in his thirty-three years in existence there was only one other person, including himself, who not only didn't find this appalling, but found it interesting and desirable. Jane. He had to find her.

"Get out," said Carol with certainty. Rusty looked at his watch. It was 7:50. He just might make it to the flower shop. "What? Do you have some place you need to be you... you jerk?"

"Yeah, actually I do," said Rusty, and he ran out of the apartment and ran straight to the flower shop. He arrived just as the owner was locking the door. Rusty had to beg him to let him in.

"It's for Jane. Please." Rusty clasped his hands together.

The owner sighed as he dropped his tired head and let Rusty in. "Only a cut flower bouquet," he said, pointing his finger in the air, as they walked back towards the flowers. "I'm not doing any arrangements. I'm done designing for the day."

"Jane isn't here?" asked Rusty.

"Nope. You're stuck with me." The flower shop owner was a 38 year old gay man who resembled a very lean, well formed gorilla in build, body hair, and facial features. He worked out frequently and was very proud of his 32 inch waist. His forearms were particularly muscular and hung down low next to his slender thighs, hands curled up almost into fists.

"Well. What kind of flowers does she like?" asked Rusty, flustered, hurried, and obviously desperate. And drunk. The flower shop owner took pity on him, sighed again, and dropped his head down to the side. What a crime it was that such a strapping young man was to be straight.

"She likes masculine flowers."

"What does that mean?" asked Rusty.

"It means Cymbidium orchids and tall grasses, but you..." the flower shop owner pointed at Rusty up and down indicating the train wreckage, "...You are going to need roses too." So the flower shop owner put together a bouquet of various kinds of orchids, tall leaning grasses and he began to cut some of the roses short, at different heights.

"Wait! Shouldn't the roses be long?" Rusty asked.

"Trust me. Your girl knows flowers. She knows they'll look better at varying heights and that they'll last longer the shorter they're cut. I know what I'm doing. Let me do my job here."

"Sorry."

"And," the owner added, "She's got this new thing now. She likes the thorns to be left on the roses. I don't know what that's all about. Should I leave them on or shave them off?" he asked, knife in hand.

Rusty smiled. "Leave them on, please."

The owner finished off the bouquet, wrapped it in tissue paper and clear cellophane and tied it off with matching ribbons of which he curled the edges.

"That'll be 75 dollars."

Rusty whistled and paid up. He walked straight to Jane's dormitory. The outside door was locked. It was cold outside. It was a weeknight and it was 8:30 now. No one was going in or out of the building. Finally, after about twenty minutes a group of three kids that all looked like they could be Jane's friends walked into the building. Rusty stood up from the stoop and asked them if they'd let him in. They refused; they didn't like the looks of him and they left him out there, flowers in hand.

Then, a pair of girls came out of the building about forty minutes later and Rusty was able to catch the door and get into the building. Rusty remembered the room and stood in front of it for a good minute, his right hand in the knocking position, his left hand holding a very expensive flower bouquet which he didn't think was very pretty. Finally he knocked.

"Just a minute!" It was Jane. There was some rustling and Jane cracked the door open just a little bit but just enough to see Rusty.

"Rusty!"

Jane stepped out of her room and closed the door behind her. She was wearing an oversized Ramones tee-shirt and nothing else. "What are you doing here?" she whispered, eyeing the flowers.

"I don't know. I mean. I'm here to see you. I missed you Jane. I was wrong. I'm so sorry." Rusty offered her the flowers. He was so sappy. Jane was taken by this. None of the guys in her circle of her friends bothered with flowers, with anything like this.

"Um. I'm sort of not alone," said Jane.

"I see," said Rusty, giving Jane the flowers. "I'll leave you be."

"No. Wait. Um. Don't go. You weren't alone tonight either." Rusty looked at Jane quizzically. "Lipstick on your mouth," Jane said, pointing to her own lips. Rusty wiped it off. "Just give me a second to break it off. Wait here." Jane went inside with the flowers, admiring them on the way in.

Rusty leaned against the wall of the dormitory, his head swimming in beer and thoughts of Jane. About fifteen minutes later a slender boy came out of Jane's room. He wore tight black jeans, black rimmed glasses, and messy hair. He looked Rusty over and smirked. Rusty was surprised by his audacity. He could have snapped the boy in half.

Jane invited Rusty in. She was dressed now.

"Thank you for the flowers. You left the thorns on." Jane smiled and turned her eyes down. "Working at a flower shop, no one ever thinks to buy you flowers." Jane hesitated. "Is this really a change of heart? You're drunk."

"Jane. I want to learn more about myself with you. I want to hold you in my arms. I want to tie you to trees. I want to take you to my mother's picnic next weekend." Rusty was being very enthusiastic.

"That's nice to hear," Jane replied, excited about the holding and tying part, not so much so about the picnic part. "But are you sure about that picnic? I'd stick out like a sore thumb."

"I don't care. I don't care because with you I can be myself. I keep going out with these other women, trying to be someone I'm not and it just doesn't work. I keep hoping that one day one of them will accept me for me, when someone already has. You. You accepted me even before I accepted myself."

"It's true," said Jane, walking over to Rusty, "I do like your freaky side." He was sitting at her desk chair facing outwards into the bedroom. She sat in his lap and wrapped her arms around his neck. "How do I know you aren't going to push me away tomorrow or the next day?"

"There's nothing I can do to prove it to you at this very moment except to not do it to you tomorrow, or the next day, or the next. Jane, I want to be with you. I want to let go of all these lies I've been telling myself all my life. I want to feel for the rest of my life the way I felt when I was with you. Powerful. Masculine." Free. Accepted.

Rusty was remarkably insightful for a drunken man. Jane knew it was not only difficult for Rusty to share these things with another human being, but difficult to admit to himself. She kissed him sweetly with her eyes closed.

She opened her eyes to see his reaction. He was still leaning forward from the kiss, his eyes starting to open. She tilted her head back and parted her lips, offering herself up to him. He grabbed her head with both hands and kissed her powerfully, deeply, massaging her scalp, messing her bright hair, running his hands around her neck and back behind her head to press it harder into his.

He stood up, grabbing Jane by her thighs and wrapping them around his waist, her arms still around his neck, and he walked over to the bed and crawled on to it. For a moment, Rusty knelt on the bed and Jane hung from him by her legs and arms, attached at the lips. He rested her on the futon mattress and began pressing her.

He pushed her arms up over her head and pressed them down into the bed at the elbows, then at the wrists, as if deciding which restraint he preferred. He had so much to learn. He pressed on her shoulders, her breasts. He pressed her legs open and down towards the bed. They didn't want to bend because Jane's jeans were so tight so he pulled the jeans down to her knees.

He felt around for her panties but found nothing. He stopped. He looked around Jane's legs to her face. She gave him a naughty smile. She wasn't wearing any panties. Rusty knew she knew he was coming in and she didn't put any on. He savagely pulled her pants off the rest of the way. She jumped onto her knees and pulled off her tee-shirt. She was naked and adorned. Rusty took off his clothes.

"I got something I think you'll like. I dunno," said Jane shrugging.

"What is it?"

"You'll see," replied Jane, innocently.

Jane was still kneeling down on the bed as she rummaged under it, left hand supporting her on the floor, right hand looking for this mysterious item. Her ass was high up in the air and Rusty could contain himself no longer.

He slapped her on the left butt cheek. Jane stopped rummaging. She put her right hand down on the ground cautiously. She raised her ass up into the air and Rusty slapped her again. Jane looked back at him; he looked at her. She nodded. He slapped her ass over and over again, Jane letting out an, "Oh my God," or an, "Ah."

When Rusty's hand hurt he stopped. He massaged Jane's ass and she returned to rummaging under the bed. As she did this Rusty stuck his fingers into her pussy, into her ass, moving them in and out, feeling the thin wall in between, feeling the wetness he had caused inside of her, feeling the skin of the openings. Finally, Jane popped up from under the bed and Rusty pulled his fingers out of her, she was smiling and a bit out of breath, holding up a pair of handcuffs.

"I thought you might like these," she said, dangling the cuffs from her forefinger. She was proud of her find yet somewhat unsure of what his response to it might be. "What do you think?"

Rusty tore into her like an animal. He grabbed the cuffs from her and pushed her onto her back. He strapped the cuffs around her neck, so that one wrist of the cuff was on one side of her neck and the other wrist was on the other side. He was pressing them into the bed, choking Jane. He tore into her mouth with his.

He kept the cuffs around her neck and nibbled at her pierced nipples, flicking his tongue at them intermittently. He kneeled up and peeled the cuffs from Jane's neck, the impression of their links still pressed into her flesh. He held them up and wondered what to do with them, what extremities shall he lock for his very own? What a wonderful gift this woman had waiting for him. He was so glad he came.

All at once Rusty knew what to do. He took Jane's left ankle and cuffed it to a slat high up on Jane's futon bed so that Jane's leg was spread open. Jane giggled and laughed at this. He was so relieved to hear this laughter. He grabbed her other leg and placed it on his chest. He lifted her pelvis up to meet his and he fucked her hard.

He fucked her so hard her breasts looked like they were going to shake off her chest. He fucked her so hard Jane had to brace herself to keep from banging her head on the bed and was only just barely successful. He fucked her so hard they both began sweating profusely and all you could hear was the pounding and slapping of muscular flesh and the occasional single minded grunt.

Rusty occasionally leaned down to bite Jane. He would fill his mouth with her side or her breast or her ear. Twice he slapped her across the face and both times she responded with open mouthed laughter which only caused Rusty to fuck her even harder. Jane began fucking Rusty back, she began grinding into him as he thrust himself into her. She became more vocal.

She began to writhe, to pull at her hair, bite her own fingers, lips. Sensing she was about to cum Rusty bit at her nipples and placed one hand over her neck to brace himself and continued fucking her in that exact same pace. She threw a complete fit, pushing his hand away, sitting up in the bed, screaming, grabbing him close with her leg, shaking her head, fucking him sitting up. Rusty could feel her insides trembling, seizing, he came too. He couldn't help it.

Rusty gently uncuffed Jane's ankle from the bed. He kissed it and laid down beside her.

"Maybe next time we could get some candles and you could pour the wax on my nipples," Jane said lightheartedly.

"Would that be nice for you?" Rusty asked, never having heard of that before.

"It sounds amazing," Jane said. "And romantic... maybe we should invest in some rope."

"Whoa. Let's not get ahead of ourselves here."

"What? You're the one asking me to your mom's picnic. I've just been doing a little bit of reading. I'm curious."

"Okay. Rope it is." Rusty hesitated. "Do you think you could wear one of those flower print dresses, that go just beneath the knee?"

"Oh my God. I have the perfect thing," said Jane, hands in the air as if to say, 'Hold on.' And she went to the closet and pulled out a vintage 1940's flower print dress. It was pink and green and had a shiny green buckle on the side of the waist. It matched her toenail polish. She pressed the dress on its hanger up against her waist and modeled it for Rusty. It was just like in the comic books. "I love vintage," she said, like the excited school girl she was.

"It's perfect," Rusty said and smiled. "Do you think you could put it on?" Jane tossed the dress over her head, zipped it most of the way, and asked Rusty to zip it the rest of the way.

"Wait," she said. And she rummaged in her closet momentarily and came out with a pair of natural leather heels. She slipped them on, combed her hair, lined her lips, and put on pink lipstick. She stretched out her arms.

"How do I look?" she asked, smiling.

"I wish we had some of that rope right now," said Rusty, walking up to her, still naked, and bending his knees so he could run his hands along the dress, along Jane's ass, her back, her breasts. He messed her hair again. He grabbed her by the head with his forefingers behind it and his thumb at her mouth and he smeared her lipstick across her face. Jane melted into his hand. Still holding onto her head he leaned down and back and grabbed the handcuffs off the bed and cuffed Jane's wrists behind her back. He pushed down on her shoulders. She knelt in front of him, facing him. He was hard again, the sight of her in that dress, the thought of her tied up in rope, willingly for him.

Jane opened her mouth and licked the tip of his cock, she licked around the ridge of its head, but she had no resistance. Her hands were cuffed behind her back. So Rusty grabbed her by the sides of her head and pushed her onto him, and off of him, and onto him again.

He pushed himself into her so deeply she gagged but when he looked down at her she continued to push her head forward. She wanted this. And with each gag more saliva came up from her throat, with each push of her head his cock became wetter and wetter until he had to pull her head off of him to keep from cumming. A trail of wetness led from her mouth to his cock as she knelt there looking up at him expectantly, proud of herself, of what she'd done to him. Rusty felt overwhelmed.

He turned her around on the carpet, burning her knees as he did so. Jane took in a "Hiss," as she inhaled. He pushed her face sideways down into the carpet so that he was pressing on her right cheek, her hands were behind her back, and her ass was in the air. He lifted her dress up to her waist.

He spit on her ass and Jane relaxed. Rusty pressed the head of his literally dripping wet cock into her ass slowly until her anus closed around it. He slid into her, his left hand still pressing on her right cheek, his right hand grabbing her thigh, pressing her onto him. He began thrusting himself into her with force, pausing in between each thrust, pushing Jane's face harder into the carpet each time.

This pace, this pose, these cuffs, this position of the dress was all very exiting to Jane and she spread her knees open along the carpet, feeling each fiber on her sore knees along the way. She could feel Rusty's balls swinging around to her clit with each thrust and with each thrust she was more aroused, more relaxed. Rusty let out a moan and suddenly began to quicken his pace, he let go of Jane's face and grabbed her with both hands by the thighs. He pounded at her ass until his pace became irregular and he thrust himself deeply into her, holding her, throbbing inside of her.

Rusty uncuffed Jane for the second time that evening, but he wasn't done with her. Out of breath, he gestured for her to touch herself. Jane felt the remains of Rusty in her pussy and now in her ass. She licked her fingers and looked up at him.

She touched her cheek; it was abraded. She touched her knees; they were abraded. She pulled hard at her nipples through the dress and hissed. Jane sat back and bent her knees up. She pulled up her dress. She stuck a finger from her left hand in her pussy, moving it in and out slowly, as if beckoning Rusty's fluids to come out. Then she stuck another finger in her pussy and began moving in and out with more rhythm.

She licked her forefinger from her right hand and began massaging her clit. This hand moved hurriedly from her clit to her nipples and back. Rusty noticed this and took over squeezing her nipples for her. He'd squeeze them hard, then pull them out, then shake them. He unbuttoned the front of her dress so he could lick her nipples and then blow on them, freezing them.

He kissed and bit her lips, her ears. Jane felt her cheek and her knees, she looked Rusty in the eyes and began moving her finger in and out of herself with greater vigor, touching her clit with more abrasion until finally her heaving and sighing became so loud Rusty covered her mouth. Her convulsing body became stiff and then limp. Rusty lifted her to the bed, laid her down, and sat next to her, running his fingers through her hair.

"I have NEVER done that in front of anyone before," said Jane.

"I've never done a lot of things before," said Rusty. "You look beautiful."

Rusty and Jane stood in front of his mother's door a week and a half later having rung the doorbell. Rusty held his chili. Jane held her cornbread.

"I didn't know you baked. I didn't even know there was an oven in your dorm. How did you even know I was making chili?"

"I have my ways. Besides, I figured chili was the only thing you could make," said Jane. She smiled at Rusty and looked at the door, waiting for it to open. Rusty eyed her as a soft breeze gently lifted the hem of her flower print dress.

THE END

Saving My Mate

Description

Tristan, an alpha, attacks and tries to subdue the rogue wolves without having any harm come to the human woman, Rhea. It is a struggle when the scent of her blood assails his nostrils and all logical thoughts flee his mind. His wolf howls in rage and ecstasy as one thought dominates his mind. A human woman is being captured and needs saving. The Alpha can't believe he has finally found his mate. In the blink of an eye, Tristan transforms into a huge coal-black wolf, his shredded clothes being the only indication that a man had stood there at all. He races forward as he watches the rogue wolf hit his mate and snarls in fury. Rhea knew who Tristan is. It takes time for her to accept the fact that she is Tristan's mate even though she finds him attractive from the first experience with him.

Chapter 1

Tristan Forest fisted his hand menacingly and snarled at the image before him. A beautiful young woman was being held tight against the body of one of the rogues while the other ran his hands down her neck and over her collarbone. The rogue's lethal claw grazed her delicate skin and the scent of her blood filled the night air, followed closely by the acrid scent of her fear. The girl struggled wildly and kicked out at the beast in front of her, landing a solid blow to his genitals. Her captor howled in fury and lashed out instantly, backhanding her face with such force that she was stunned by the blow and hung her head forward limply.

Tristan had been contemplating how best to subdue the rogue wolves without having any harm come to the human woman when the scent of her blood assailed his nostrils and all logical thought fled his mind. His wolf howled in rage and ecstasy as one thought dominated his mind. MINE!! The Alpha couldn't believe he had finally found his mate. In the blink of an eye, Tristan transformed into a huge coal-black wolf, his shredded clothes being the only indication that a man had stood there at all. He raced forward as he watched the rogue hit his mate and snarled in fury.

The rogues looked up startled at the black blur racing toward them and dropped the girl quickly, taking off toward the woods. Tristan howled again as he was torn between chasing after them and checking on his mate. His protective instincts won out and he ran to her, transforming into his human form mid-stride.

Rhea Blake swore under her breath as she shook her head to dispel the dizziness that had engulfed her for a moment after the man/animal thing had hit her. She watched in fascination as the huge black wolf morphed into a man just a few feet away from her and sucked in a breath at the gorgeous image that met her eyes. He was the most stunning thing she had ever laid her eyes on. Tall and firmly muscled with short dark hair and piercing emerald green eyes, the mystery man looked at her in concern before crouching down beside her. Rhea blushed as she realized he was stark naked and focused on his face to stop her eyes from drifting downward to what she was sure would be an impressive sight.

"Are you all right Little One?" he asked worriedly, fighting his instinct to gather her up in his arms and carry her off to claim her primitively.

"Uhm, yes, I'm fine, thank you," she responded cautiously.

"You were hit pretty hard. Can you stand up?"

"Yes, I'm sure I can," she said while trying to get to her feet. Rhea swayed as the world spun and then gasped as she felt strong arms encircling her body, making her dizzy for a different reason entirely.

"It's all right, I've got you," the stranger said comfortingly. "I'm Tristan Forest. What's your name?" he enquired, while guiding her to her car. Tristan gazed into the beautiful hazel brown eyes of his mate and tenderly brushed aside a lock of her wavy chestnut colored hair.

"Rhea. Rhea Blake," she answered.

"You have a beautiful name, Rhea."

"T-thank you," she stuttered.

"Let me get you to a hospital Little One so that we can have you checked out, okay?"

"What? No, that won't be necessary," she said. "Look I'm really grateful you scared them off but I'm fine and I don't think it would be smart to go anywhere with a naked werewolf right now," she said bluntly.

Tristan stared at his mate in shock. She knew what he was? Why wasn't she freaking out? Rhea looked into his eyes and almost laughed at the comical confused expression that was apparent in his strong features.

"Don't look so surprised Mr. Forest. It would hardly take a rocket scientist to figure it out. The idiots who attacked me sprouted claws and fur out of nowhere and you transformed from a wolf to a man in front of my very eyes. That's pretty solid evidence of what you are."

Tristan continued to stare at her, dumbfounded by her easy acceptance of all she had seen. Then common sense took over and his usual confident self-assurance shone through.

"Okay, so you figured out what we are. That doesn't change the fact that you were hit pretty hard and you're still bleeding. I'm going to fetch some clothes and take you to the hospital. And please call me Tristan," he ordered.

"No. Thank you for your concern, Tristan but no. I can take care of myself. I just need to replace this tire and I'll be good to go," she said decisively.

Tristan frowned at his mate's stubbornness and realised that trying to convince her would get him nowhere. He had to be clever about this.

"At least let me sort that out for you then Rhea. I'll put on some clothes first if it will make you more comfortable," he teased with a cocky grin.

Rhea sighed and decided to just let him sort out the tire. He obviously wasn't going to just let her leave and she did feel a bit woozy still.

"All right Tristan. But where are you going to find clothes now? In your hidden den?" she asked somewhat sarcastically.

Tristan grinned in response. "No, my sweet, it's just beyond the trees. Give me a second."

Rhea watched as he ran off toward the greenery and disappeared into the dense foliage. She had a feeling that

Tristan Forest was going to be trouble, in the most delicious of ways. She had to be wary with him or she knew she would be falling hard for him before she could even catch her breath.

Rhea watched as Tristan jogged back to her in just a pair of loose jeans. She was surprised that he had actually found a pair of jeans in the forest but she figured werewolves thought ahead about these things. He was much taller than she was, probably around 6'3 and he oozed strength and masculinity. Her eyes were drawn to his defined abs and pectoral muscles and she immediately felt the urge to run her hands and her tongue over every inch of his body. Rhea blushed at the direction her thoughts were traveling in. She was still a virgin at twenty-four years old and had never been interested in anything physical with a man before. Granted, Tristan was not just a man, but he was still a stranger who had suddenly awoken primal thoughts and urges within her and she didn't know what to make of it.

Tristan gazed at his mate as he jogged toward her and noticed that she was lost in thought. He took the opportunity to absorb every detail about her that he could. She was of average height for a woman, around 5'6 but not petite. She had long wavy brown hair that he itched to run his hands through and a curvy figure. Tristan had to fight the urge to groan aloud as she bit her bottom lip while she was thinking and he finally met her heated hazel eyes before she blinked and seemed to shake herself back to the present. He jealously wondered what she had been thinking about that caused her to get that sexy intense expression on her face and decided to get to the task of changing her tire before he started demanding that she divulge every thought that passed through her mind.

"Pop the trunk my sweet. I'll need to get the jack and the spare tire."

Rhea did as he asked and then watched as he quickly and efficiently replaced her blown out tire with the spare one. Within minutes the car was ready to move.

"Thank you, Tristan. I appreciate your help," she said sincerely.

"It was a pleasure Rhea. Now let's get you to the hospital."

"Tristan, for the tenth time, I'm fine. I really don't need the hospital. And I'll be there later on anyway. So I'll get looked at then, okay?" she said somewhat impatiently.

"Why will you be there later on? Are you all right?" he demanded.

"Yes, I'm fine. I work there. I'm a nurse, which is how I know I'm fine. Is there anything else you need to know?" she asked sarcastically. Rhea wondered why she was being so prickly with him and then realised that it was because she was so intrinsically drawn to this man that it scared her. Everything about him called to her and she hated the fact that she actually liked his demanding tone and the way he seemed to expect obedience.

The easiest way to deal with it was sarcasm and anger. She wasn't naive enough to imagine that this divine creature would actually be interested in her so it would be safer for her to just part ways with him now and keep her heart secure from any possible future pain.

Tristan grinned at her annoyed tone before replying, "Just one other thing. What time do you get off work?"

"Noon," Rhea answered distractedly.

"I'll see you then Little One."

Rhea cursed herself for being so preoccupied and actually telling him the correct time that her shift would end but then realized that he would not know which hospital she worked at anyway. Nonetheless, she wouldn't be encouraging him regardless of how quickly he set her pulse racing.

"Look, I appreciate your help Tristan but I don't think it would be a good idea for us to socialize. You seem like a great guy and everything but there would be no point to us becoming friends."

Rhea looked up into his twinkling eyes and her breath caught in her throat even as she dreaded his response.

"I don't just want to be friends with you Rhea," he said in a deep voice full of promise. "You will be mine whether you know it yet or not."

Ignoring the fact that her heart had literally just skipped a beat, Rhea narrowed her eyes and got into her car. "We'll see about that Mr. Forest. Have a good evening."

Chapter 2

Before Tristan could stop her, Rhea started the car and drove off. She kept her eyes on him for as long as possible before breathing a sigh of relief and trying to calm her erratic heartbeat. She had no idea what Tristan had meant by his possessive words and she had no intention of finding out. Even if he did, by some miracle, come to the right hospital, she would not allow herself to be drawn in by him. She would be a notch on Tristan's bedpost no matter how much he drew her in.

Having resolved to avoid Tristan at all costs, Rhea headed home to shower before starting her shift. She worked odd hours at the hospital, taking the shifts that everyone else tended to avoid. Rhea had nobody to spend her free time with and wasn't inclined to meet new people since she had learned from experience that the people closest to you had the ability to hurt you the most. So, she instead focused her time and energy on the children in the pediatric ward of the Forest Hospital and it was by far the most fulfilling aspect of her life. Children were still innocent and loving without having ulterior motives.

Rhea loved the simplicity in the way kids thought. It was so much easier dealing with them as opposed to the endless mindless games adults played.

Rhea arrived home a few minutes later and allowed her mind to wander as she stepped into the shower, ignoring the throbbing heat between her legs that had been caused by Tristan's intense unwavering stare and sculpted muscles. The man exuded a powerful sexuality that Rhea could not help but react to and she wished that she had enough time to relieve the ache he had caused. But she had to get to her shift on time. So she brutally squashed the urge to bring herself to orgasm and proceeded to wash her hair instead.

Rhea had been happy, or at least as close as she could get, until meeting Tristan Forest. She knew she wasn't frigid or jilted. She had chosen to live her life without getting close to people for a good reason. But now Rhea found herself questioning her choices and her lonely existence. Tristan had unknowingly caused her to become dissatisfied with the course her life was on. She wondered how one man could have such a profound effect on her after one simple encounter.

Frowning as she got dressed in her simple blue scrubs and tennis shoes, Rhea thought about how she had gotten to this point in her life. She had been a happy child for the first few years of her life. Then things just went downhill and had never picked back up. Rhea considered everything she had been through a learning experience and so she had no regrets. That didn't stop her from wishing things had been different. She shook herself out of her funk, determined to not allow herself to become even more depressed than usual and left for work.

Rhea hoped that the day would bring would bring no further surprises. As much as she would love to see Tristan again, she knew that it would only lead to further heartache and she didn't know how much more of that she could take. Groaning aloud at the fact that her thoughts had once again returned to Tristan, Rhea prayed silently that she could forget him and the electrifying effect he seemed to have on her mind and her body.

***Tristan watched as Rhea drove off and chuckled at the way she had politely tried to get him to back off. He could tell that his mate was a feisty one and that he would have to be persistent with her. There was no way he would forget she existed. It simply wasn't an option. Tristan shifted into his wolf form and followed Rhea's car from a distance. He ran along the periphery of the woods and easily kept track of her all theway to her little cottage. He was surprised by the fact that she lived so close to the woods. He knew that that particular cottage was hardly ever occupied due to people being afraid of the occasional wild animal heard in the forest.

Tristan growled at the thought that his mate had been so close to the pack's compound all this time and he had not once scented her. He was usually very level-headed but his wolf was impatient to mate with Rhea and he could find no compelling reason to hold the wolf at bay. His mate seemed to be fine with the idea of werewolves so all he needed to do was convince her that they were in fact soul mates and were destined to be together. It was that simple. Tristan groaned, knowing that this task was far easier said than done.

His thoughts were disturbed by the sound of running water and Tristan let out a strangled groan at the image of Rhea taking a shower. He could picture the water flowing smoothly over her naked smooth creamy skin and he shut his eyes in a futile attempt to escape the picture his mind had conjured up. Tristan waited a little while longer until he saw his mate exit the cottage and leave for work, his wolf only calm because he knew they would be seeing their mate later on that day.

Tristan sprinted back to the pack's compound to inform his betas that there would soon be an alpha female joining the ranks and to prepare for his meeting with Rhea. He was ecstatic and could hardly process the fact that he had actually found his life mate.

Tristan had waited for four hundred years and had been contemplating the idea that he just was not destined to find his mate. It was a ridiculous notion but he had watched many of his family and friends' mate with the one special person that fate had gifted them with while he remained alone. Now he had found his destiny and he knew that he had to tread carefully. Failure was not an option. Tristan linked telepathically to Aidan, his second in command, as he neared the compound.

Aidan, are you at the compound or at work?

I'm still at work Alpha. Am I needed at the compound? I'll leave immediately.

Oh cut the Alpha crap. We've been best friends for three centuries. I just have a question. Is there a Rhea Blake working at the hospital?

Yes there is. She's a nurse in pediatrics and she lives at that cottage on the south side of our border. Why do you ask Tris?

She's my mate Aid!! I've finally found her!! I can't believe she's been living near the compound and working at the hospital all this time and I never knew she was so close.

Well we know there's no such thing as coincidence brother. There must be a good reason why your meeting was delayed and I'm sure we'll find out soon enough. You know, this might not go down too well with the other females in the pack. They've been trying to get your attention for years and they won't take this too kindly. Not to mention the fact that she's human.

Yes I know there are some who won't be pleased but any disagreement will have to go through me. Besides, the mate that Luna gifted to me would not be meek and submissive. I know she'll be able to handle herself. I'm briefing the other betas in a few minutes. So I'll see what the reaction is like then.

Tristan closed off his mental link to Aidan as he shifted back into human form and entered his private living quarters. He took a quick shower and changed into a pair of black cargo pants and a plain black t-shirt before linking telepathically to his three other betas and calling a quick meeting in his study. The betas were in charge of various duties.

They were all fierce warriors but were also given great responsibility in helping Tristan rule the pack and the numerous corporations owned by them. Unlike most other wolf packs, Tristan had female betas as well as male and he trusted them all implicitly. He watched from the window as all three arrived at his cabin at the same time and smiled as Caden opened the door for the two women, Katrina and Alyssa. Tristan was unfailingly proud of the fact that all the men in his pack treated women with courtesy and respect, regardless of rank.

"Thank you all for heeding my call. This won't be long. I just have an announcement and then you all can return to whatever you were doing."

All three nodded and stood waiting for Tristan to continue.

"I have found my mate and will hopefully be bringing her to the compound soon. There may be issues with certain members of the pack since she is human. So I want you all to be aware and keep your ears open to any possible threat. I will not tolerate her being harmed by any other person, especially any pack members."

"T-man that's great news!! Wow!! I'm so happy for you!!" Caden congratulated Tristan. The tall sandy haired giant smiled cheekily while he clasped forearms with Tristan and thumped his back in the traditional way of greeting.

The two women expressed similar reactions and wished Tristan well in his pursuit of his mate. Tristan thanked them all and asked Caden to stay behind while he dismissed the two women.

"Cal I want you to be extra vigilant. I trust Kat and Alyssa but I know they might hesitate if their friends or family show dissent. I want you to be my right hand on this."

"Sure thing Alpha. Thank you for entrusting me with this. You know I won't let you down."

The two men shook hands before Caleb left Tristan's cabin. Tristan grabbed his car keys as soon as he was alone and headed off to the hospital, eager to see his mate once again.

***

Rhea found herself lost in thought more than once during her shift and mentally shook herself for her distraction. It had never happened to her before as she was always aware of her surroundings, especially at work. She cursed Tristan for invading her thoughts and focused on the files she was organizing. It was the worst part of her shift, the hour before she got off duty.

Rhea turned to grab the last file off the desk and gasped as she came face to face with Aidan Forest. The man was beautiful in a severe somber sort of way with short brown hair and piercing icy blue eyes. Rhea placed her hand on her throat in surprise at his sudden appearance. She was not at all used to being caught unaware and it was the second time in less than 24 hours that she had managed to get into an odd situation without even seeing any sign of it coming. The werewolves that had accosted her on the road had literally appeared out of nowhere and by the time Rhea realized that she was not alone they were too close for her to escape.

Rhea gazed at Aidan and briefly wondered at her complete lack of interest in him before she spoke. "I'm sorry Mr. Forest, I didn't realize you were there. Is there anything I can help you with?" she asked politely.

"No nurse Blake, not really. And please, call me Aidan. I've just come to inform you that another nurse has come in early so you may end your shift now, if you wish."

Rhea frowned as she wondered why the head surgeon would feel the need to inform her of shift changes but shrugged off the weird feeling before replying.

"It's just Rhea. And thank you for letting me know Aidan. I'll clock out now then. Have a good day."

"I'll walk you to the foyer Nurse Blake," Aidan said formally.

Rhea saw no way out of the situation without being rude and she really did not want to offend Aidan Forest of all people so she sighed in capitulation and walked to the staff changing room to collect her bag and change into her everyday sneakers. She emerged from the room half expecting Aidan to have disappeared but found him waiting in the exact position he had been in when she walked into the staff room. Rhea followed the imposing man to the elevator and wondered whether she should attempt to chat with him but dismissed the idea after glancing at his stony features. The man was the youngest and most successful heart surgeon in the country but he definitely needed to lighten up.

Rhea was so lost in thought that she was startled when the elevator bell chimed, signaling that it was at the hospital foyer. She turned to thank Aidan for escorting her but he had already turned away and was heading to the receptionist's desk. Rhea frowned at his odd behavior before slinging her bag diagonally across her shoulders and heading to the stairwell that led to the employees' parking facilities. She was suddenly shoved from the right and swore under her breath as she waited to feel the impact of hitting the porcelain tiles that decorated the foyer floor. After a few seconds Rhea forced her eyes open and gasped as her gaze was instantly snared by the half-irritated, half-amused emerald green eyes that had haunted her since last night. She groaned as he began speaking and she became aware of his strong arms wrapped around her.

"We've got to stop meeting like this my sweet," he grinned.

"Tell that to the idiot who decided I should become intimately acquainted with the floor. What are you doing here Tristan?"

"I told you I'd see you after your shift Rhea and I am a man of my word."

"You know, this could be considered stalking. What did you do, call every hospital in the city?"

"Nope, I just called Aidan," Tristan replied seriously.

Rhea glanced at him as if he was certifiable before the realisation of what he said actually sunk in.

"That snake!! That's why he randomly decided to escort me downstairs. He knew you'd be here!"

Tristan growled at the idea of Rhea being alone with an unmated male and his gaze turned feral as his wolf insisted, they mark their territory so every male would know that Rhea belonged to them.

"Okay really now, is the growling necessary?" she asked impatiently.

"Huh?" Tristan looked completely taken aback.

"What's with the growling under your breath? You're making the sick people uneasy."

Tristan looked around and realized that a few people were staring at him and Rhea.

"I don't like the idea of you being alone with any other male. Now you must be starving, I'm taking you to lunch Little One."

"What? Are you insane? Any other male? My God, why do I attract the loony ones? You show up at my work like a crazy stalker person and expect me to just come along with you? I don't think so Tristan. You must be out of your freaking—"

Rhea's tirade was suddenly cut off by the high-pitched squeak of her head nurse. Rhea winced at the sound before realizing that Nurse Stone was headed rapidly toward her and Tristan.

"Mr. Forest, oh what a pleasure to see you here, sir! We weren't expecting you today. Let me escort you to your office or is there anything else you would like me to help with?" she gushed.

Rhea frowned at the enthusiastic enthralled tone coming from one of the scariest women on the planet. Tristan had to school his features so as to not laugh at his mate's obvious irritation.

"No thank you Nurse Stone. I'm just here to pick up my lunch date so that won't be necessary."

The large imposing woman's eyebrows shot up in surprise and she looked at Rhea for the first time since spotting Tristan. An expression of disbelief crossed her face before she turned back to Tristan.

"Lunch date? Well then let me know who the lucky lady is and I'll send Rhea here to fetch her for you."

"Actually, Rhea is my date Nurse Stone and I do believe I am the lucky one in the situation," Tristan said coolly. "That is if she would grace me with her presence," he teased Rhea.

Rhea was fuming at her supervisor's audacity and decided to play the situation up a bit. Nurse Stone always had it in for Rhea and now was her chance to exact her revenge. Ignoring the other woman's presence, Rhea saddled up to Tristan and looked him up and down as if considering what he had to offer.

"Oh, I'm not so sure Tristan. I mean I have quite a busy schedule today. I don't think there's enough time to fit you in," she said almost regretfully. Before Tristan could reply Nurse Stone cut in with an incensed gasp.

"Are you out of your mind?? Have some respect you insolent woman!! Don't you know who Mr Forest is!!??"

Chapter 3

Rhea tried not to laugh aloud at the irate shocked tone of Nurse Stone's voice as she chastised her for being so brazen. "I'm certain you'll be enlightening me on the topic..."

"You should be ashamed of yourself woman! How dare you be so disrespectful! I'll have you fired for your impertinence! Tristan Forest is the owner of Forest Industries and a great benefactor to this hospital. You should be honored that he even noticed you exist!" Nurse Stone almost shouted.

The thought that the head nurse might be perilously close to bursting a blood vessel crossed Rhea's mind before she replied, "If you must know, I am completely aware of who he is, Nurse Stone. And you can't fire me. You wouldn't know how to deal with the children otherwise. Now if you'll both excuse me, I have somewhere else I need to be."

With that said, Rhea turned and began walking once again to the stairwell. She became aware of a presence behind her and turned to face Tristan, not realizing how close behind her he actually was.

"Oomph!" she squeaked out as she almost collided with his strong frame. "Oh, dear Lord. For goodness sake, leave me alone you insufferable man," she said exasperatedly.

"Oh, no you don't. What do you mean you know exactly who I am? Why didn't you say anything? And why are you so hell bent on avoiding spending any time with me?" Tristan demanded.

" I don't have to explain anything to you," Rhea bit out tersely.

"Maybe not, but I'll get the answers out of you anyway," Tristan said with a decidedly predatory glint in his eyes.

"Try your worst Tristan, I'm not afraid of you," Rhea lied. She had no idea why she was being so evasive with him but her defenses were up big time and she always trusted her instincts. Although this time she wasn't certain exactly what she was afraid of. She just knew that the safest thing to do would be to run and not look back.

Tristan paused as he saw the lie in her eyes and heard her heart pounding harshly. His mate was afraid of him? He let go of her slowly and backed away, running a frustrated hand through his hair. Tristan had been tempering his usual dominant streak around Rhea but she was still afraid of him. The thought made his stomach clench and he wondered if he should give her more time and be less persistent. Perhaps she would be more amenable to spending time with him if he took things a lot slower. Tristan's train of thought was broken by a hesitant touch on his forearm and he looked into Rhea's confused, worried eyes.

"What's wrong?" she asked tentatively.

Rhea found herself becoming more and more concerned as Tristan had stood a few feet away from her running his hand through his hair. She knew that it would be the ideal time to walk to the parking lot quietly and just leave, but he looked almost defeated and the image did not sit well with her. Before she could stop herself, she realized that she had reached out to touch him. The spark she felt beneath her fingertips almost made Rhea gasp aloud, but she tempered her reaction and focused on his eyes instead.

Tristan took hold of Rhea's hand and placed a gentle kiss on her palm before replying. "Absolutely nothing, my sweet. I am truly sorry that I've caused you to become afraid of me. I haven't courted a human before and I suppose I'm doing it all wrong with you. I'll let you go home now if that's what you want."

Rhea read the sadness in his eyes and she felt her heart constrict at the thought that she had made him feel that way. Rhea was vaguely aware that she seemed to be in no control of her emotions at all but didn't question the sudden change of heart. She just knew with every fiber of her being that she could not ever hurt the gorgeous man in front of her. So she made a decision and hoped it would not backfire.

"You know, I could use a sandwich or something. Where are we going?" she asked.

"You don't have to come with me under duress, Rhea. I don't want you to feel obligated in any way, Little One," Tristan said although he was praying fervently that she did not take back her acceptance.

"I'm not under duress. I'm hungry. Now, lead on oh great benefactor," she teased.

Tristan chuckled before gallantly offering her his arm and they began walking out the hospital's front sliding doors. Rhea knew that her pulse was racing, although this time it was more in anticipation than fear. She hated how inconsistent she was being but decided she'd just go with her gut from now on.

"So are you going to tell me how you knew who I was?" Tristan asked casually.

Rhea grinned broadly before replying, "It would hardly take a rocket scientist to figure it out. Your name is legend and you had Aidan Forest, grouch extraordinaire, informed me that my shift was over. I just put two and two together."

Tristan led Rhea to a coal black '69 Camaro and unlocked the passenger door for her. "Oh wow! This is yours?" Rhea asked excitedly. "It's gorgeous!"

"Yep, she's mine. I restored her myself. I take it you like American muscle cars then, Little One?"

"It's a guilty pleasure. I've never owned one, but I love them. Show me what she can do Tristan. "

Tristan nearly groaned aloud at the excited husky timber of his mate's voice and clenched his fist as she let out a soft breathy moan when he started the engine and it hummed to life. Part of him was jealous of her reaction to the car and he grinned wryly at the thought that he was envious of an inanimate object.

Tristan drove fast but he was completely in control and Rhea loved every second. She was reluctant to leave the car when Tristan parked outside a little cafe and sighed regretfully before taking his hand and allowing him to help her step out of the amazing piece of machinery.

"You know, I should be hurt that you're already so in love with the car but won't even eat lunch with me without kicking up a fuss," Tristan sighed teasingly although there was an odd note in his voice.

Rhea blushed before mumbling, "I wouldn't be so hurt if I were you Tristan, you severely underestimate your appeal."

Tristan felt his wolf rumble its approval at the hint of their attraction being mutual and he felt himself cornering Rhea against the car without even thinking about what he was doing. Tristan placed his hands on the frame of the door and leaned forward until he was in contact with his mate from knee to chest. Her shocked gasp made him smile and he gazed at her expressive face as she resembled a startled deer caught in the headlights of an oncoming eighteen-wheeler.

Rhea keenly felt every inch of Tristan that was pressed so tightly against her body and her pulse raced as her skin tingled from the contact. Half of her prayed that he would kiss her and the other half prayed that she was dreaming and would wake up any minute. Rhea found his dominance unbelievably arousing and she was extremely aware of her lack of experience when it came to relationships. She was suddenly afraid that she would seem like a naive adolescent in the face of Tristan's overpowering sexuality and whimpered in panic before looking up into his piercing emerald green eyes.

Uh oh, Rhea though belatedly as she became ensnared in his powerful gaze. Tristan knew that Rhea was overthinking everything and decided to drag her attention back to the present. He looked deeply into her surprised hazel eyes before lowering his head ever so slowly. Rhea held her breath as Tristan's face came nearer and nearer to hers and let out a small gasp as he slowly licked along her trembling lower lip. She felt a surge of heat at the intimacy and grabbed his t-shirt to steady her trembling limbs.

Tristan had to fight everything within him not to just grab her and take her somewhere private to ravish her senseless. That brief taste of her had his head spinning and he shut his eyes while touching his forehead to hers in an attempt to cool his blood. Rhea whimpered again. This time at the loss of contact, and lifted her mouth to find his before her inhibitions took over. Tristan groaned as Rhea's lips met his softly and tentatively and the battle for self-control was lost. He pulled her against his body more tightly and took control of the kiss, pressing his mouth firmly against hers and teasing her with little swipes of his tongue against the seam of her lips. Rhea gasped as Tristan gently bit into her lower lip and he took advantage by claiming her mouth fully and forcefully with his talented tongue.

Rhea felt as if the world was spinning as Tristan asserted his dominance in the most pleasurable of ways. She was amazed at how easy it was to just lose herself in his intoxicating taste. He reminded her of the decadent flavor of dark chocolate and she could gladly stay like this with him forever. Tristan felt his wolf howl in joy and pride as their mate submitted to him willingly. He traced her teeth with his tongue before drawing hers out almost playfully. Tristan suddenly broke the kiss and pressed his forehead against hers once more.

"You sorely test my self-control, my sweet, but we are about to be interrupted and I don't think this particular interruption will be very tactful about the situation. But trust me, we will be continuing this later," he promised.

Rhea's fuzzy brain took a few seconds to comprehend what Tristan was saying and then she blushed a deep red before burying her face in his t-shirt and groaning aloud.

Rhea groaned again and pushed futilely at Tristan's chest to try to get him to move. He didn't budge and she would have been cussing him out if it weren't for the fact that his kiss had left her reeling and she was totally off kilter. She couldn't believe that she had been so brazen.

"In a hurry, Rhea?" Tristan asked lazily.

"No, I told you, I'm hungry. Now move," she demanded, finally finding her voice and her self-respect.

Tristan chuckled but stepped back and grabbed her hand to lead her into the cafe, extremely pleased at her response to their first kiss and elated that she had practically initiated it. He opened the door for Rhea and then led her to a booth in the corner nearest to the door. The cafe was quite busy but the noise quieted down as a number of people averted their eyes when Tristan walked past.

"Oh Lord!" Rhea suddenly said softly, standing up and grabbing her purse. "You're an Alpha aren't you? Jesus!! I am so outta here!!"

Tristan looked at her in shock before gripping her wrist to stop her from running away.

"Rhea, please sit down. I will explain anything you want to know but don't ever run from me, Little One."

Rhea registered Tristan's very serious expression and decided self-preservation would be better served by her sitting down and doing whatever he told her to, until the opportunity to get away presented itself.

"Yes, I am the Alpha of the Forest Pack. How did you guess?"

"You're the owner of Forest Industries, you get to order Aidan around, people stop talking and look down when you walk past them and you just command respect. It's not exactly how betas and omegas behave. Look Tristan, whatever it is you want from me, just tell me now so you can save yourself the effort of pretending to court me or whatever and just get on with business," she said flatly.

"What on earth are you talking about, woman? I'm not pretending to do anything. And how in Luna's name do you know so much about us?" Tristan asked in frustration. His mate was making no sense and he hated feeling so uncertain.

"Tristan, just tell me what you want. Don't play games. I can handle the truth. And I just know these things, okay? Now please just—"

Rhea's speech was cut short by Tristan. "Dammit Rhea, I want you! You are my mate. We were destined to be together. Do you understand the concept of life-mates when it comes to wolves?"

Rhea suddenly stiffened as her gaze fell past Tristan to the doorway of the cafe and she stared in growing horror as panic engulfed her like a tidal wave.

"Oh, hell no, I am not going through this again. Whatever sick game you're playing Mr. Forest, count me out. I've had enough drama with bloody werewolves to last me a lifetime."

Tristan became aware of the bitter scent of her fear and panic. This time he knew it was not directed at him and his wolf growled at the idea that something was causing such terror in their mate. He looked up and his wolf surged fiercely at the image of the man in the doorway of the cafe. He growled under his breath and stood up immediately, barely registering the members of his pack who did the same and moved into defensive positions around his booth.

"Tristan!" the stranger boomed. "It's good to see you again, brother. "

Tristan stood so still that Rhea thought he resembled a stone statue. She would have been more puzzled by his reaction if she weren't freaking out over the fact that her worst nightmare had just walked into the cafe and addressed Tristan as "brother." She should have known that she could never escape his horrific clutches. It was too much to hope that she would be able to live a normal productive supernatural-free life.

"What, no warm embrace? I'm hurt brother," the stranger laughed.

"What do you want Logan? You aren't welcome in this territory and you are no brother of mine," Tristan said coldly.

"Ooh, that one hurt. Can't a guy just stop by to check how his little brother is doing?"

"No. Now leave before I'm forced to remove you."

Logan's cold-black eyes flitted to Rhea and a slow smirk spread across his face.

"Just hand over the hot brunette you have over there Tristan and I'll be on my way. It's not nice to keep a man's property from him," Logan said jovially.

Tristan saw red with those words and had to reign in every instinct he possessed to not rip off Logan's head where he stood.

"It would serve you well to never so much as glance in her direction again Logan. I won't be as lenient with you as I was the last time," Tristan bit out.

Logan's eyes hardened at the reminder of what had transpired between them the last time they saw each other.

"I would have thought you'd avoid interfering with mates Tristan. You know the sacred law. And Rhea over there is most definitely my mate," Logan said cheerfully.

Tristan heard Rhea whimper almost inaudibly and his deadly claws slid out slowly, a clear warning to his brother. There was no way in hell he would be letting him take Rhea. She was HIS mate. Nobody else would be touching her.

"I believe you are sorely mistaken Logan. Rhea belongs to no other wolf but me. You should know better than to quote sacred law to me. Now leave," Tristan said, surprised by how calm he sounded.

"In that case I challenge you to the right to mate with her, brother dearest," Logan growled, clearly displeased with Tristan's claim on Rhea.

"I gladly accept. Now get your scruffy horde the hell off my land before my betas are forced to teach your pack a lesson about the meaning of territory," Tristan growled.

"We will meet again soon Tristan," Logan promised.

Chapter 4

Tristan watched his brother's pack file out of the cafe and he fought the urge to roar at their traitorous impudence. Tristan was the Alpha by right and by strength and he itched to get the fight with his brother done right then and there. Suddenly aware once more of the scent of fear surrounding his mate. Tristan turned sharply, just in time to see Rhea sliding quietly out of the booth.

"Oh no you don't," Tristan bit out, lifting her up and placing her over his shoulder. "I want answers, mate, and I want them now."

Tristan's overwhelming instinct at that moment was to take Rhea somewhere private and claim her in the primitive way of the wolves but his Alpha responsibilities dictated that he finds out exactly why his brother believed Rhea was his mate and why he had dared to resurface in Tristan's territory after all these years. Tristan was pissed beyond belief but he reigned in his wolf and walked out to his car.

"Put me down Tristan, please. I promise I won't say a thing. I'll leave the area and be gone for good. Please, I'm begging you, just let me go."

Tristan registered the note of hysteria in her voice and put her down gently as he reached his car, despite the rage simmering in him. Ignoring the look of relief on Rhea's face, he opened the passenger side door and waited for her to get in.

Rhea thought for a brief second that he was letting her go but then she saw the steely look in his eyes as he waited for her to get into the car and felt her hopes get crushed with that one look. She got in quietly and shuffled as close to the door as possible after he walked to the driver's side. She didn't dare try to run at that moment because she knew he would catch her before she even got out of the car. Rhea registered Tristan's clenched fists and rigid jaw before he got into the driver's seat.

She shut her eyes and prayed fervently that this was just a bad dream and that she was sleeping safely in her home. She refused to acknowledge the fact that Logan had just marched back into her life, that he was Tristan's brother and that they were apparently going to fight over the right to claim her. Rhea felt herself being dragged into memories she swore to forget a long time ago and shivered unconsciously as she kept her eyes shut, trying her hardest to think of how she could escape from Tristan.

Rhea's train of thought was interrupted by the feeling of the car coming to a stop. She blinked her eyes open and watched warily as Tristan opened the passenger side door for her.

"Come on Little one. You're safe here. This is my home."

Rhea scoffed at his promise that she was safe but exited the car quietly and walked up the steps leading to the front door. The cabin was huge and she could tell that although it looked rustic, there was plenty of high tech security surrounding the house.

Tristan opened the front door and watched Rhea carefully for her reaction to her future home. Despite his anger and the drama of the last half an hour, he was still anxious about her seeing their home for the first time.

Rhea kept her expression carefully blank as she surveyed her surroundings. The house was clean and neat but still very homely. She could easily envisage sitting in front of the fireplace wrapped tightly in Tristan's strong arms, watching their children play a few feet away.

Whoa woman! Get a grip. Your life is in danger. Again. Don't be fooled by a bloody werewolf, Rhea mentally chastised herself.

Tristan hated the fact that Rhea could so easily hide her feelings from him. He couldn't tell if she was pleased by his home or not but he knew that there were more pressing matters at hand.

"Rhea," he began, "I'm not going to hurt you sweetheart. I need to know why Logan thinks you are his mate."

Rhea cringed at the mention of that monster's name but she analyzed the events that occurred in the cafe and came to the conclusion that either Tristan and Logan truly despised each other, or they were both amazing actors. Her throat ached at the idea that Tristan was as evil as his brother but she decided that she would not volunteer any information until she knew for sure what Tristan's motives were. Her paranoia had served her well in the past and even though her instinct told her that Tristan could be trusted, logic prevailed and forced her to say nothing.

Tristan could see the wheels turning in Rhea's head. After a few minutes of silence he realized she planned on ignoring his question. He ran his hands through his hair in frustration and thought about how he could persuade her to talk. His wolf was extremely agitated that his brother had interacted with his mate before Tristan had found her and her terror at seeing Logan had Tristan's imagination running through the worst possible scenarios. He felt his eyes shift into the inky black of his wolf and his claws cut through the air slowly. Tristan had to fight every urge in his body as his wolf wrestled him for dominance. He felt cold fury as he recalled Rhea's expression at seeing Logan. Beads of sweat gathered on Tristan's forehead as he fought his beast for control.

Rhea watched in fascination as Tristan's eyes changed color, the piercing black making him look dark and deadly. She was shaken out of her funk when his claws slid out and she realized that he was fighting his beast. For some reason, Rhea wasn't afraid of this side of Tristan. She knew to be careful but every instinct in her was urging her to try and calm him down.

Rhea approached him slowly and lifted her hand up to his jaw. Her skin tingled at the contact and her breath hitched but she was determined to bring him back.

"Tristan... Come back to me," she urged quietly.

Tristan was losing himself. He could feel the wolf gaining dominance and pushed harder to regain control. Distantly he realized Rhea had approached him and at her timid touch on his jaw he felt the wolf recede abruptly. He shook his head as if to clear it and realized the wolf had lost its rabid fury as soon as he realized they were possibly endangering their mate.

"Oh Luna! Rhea, forgive me Little One. I can't stand the thought of you being hurt and my wolf wants to find Logan and shred him to pieces. I'm so sorry I lost control like that," Tristan said, unable to meet her eyes.

Rhea cupped his jaw more fully and lifted his head so that his eyes met hers. She could see the self-loathing in his eyes but also the anger boiling beneath the surface. Rhea couldn't tell if Tristan was just acting or not but she realized that she truly believed he was being sincere. His reactions were just too primal and spontaneous to be deceptive.

"It's okay. I'm okay. Look, I still don't know whether this is the wisest move but I'll tell you whatever you need to know. For whatever bizarre reason, I trust you Tristan," Rhea said softly.

Tristan felt immense relief as Rhea spoke and then felt his wolf howl happily at her indication that she trusted them. His eyes flared and he stared at her intensely without uttering a word.

Rhea felt more self-conscious the longer Tristan stared at her. The forceful penetrating expression in his gaze made her feel hot and cold all at once and she pulled her hands away from his face abruptly, letting out a nervous breath as she did so. She couldn't believe how bold she was around him and how he so easily made her forget herself. Just five minutes ago she had doubted everything about him and wanted to run as far away as possible and now she wanted nothing more than to have him touch her and never let go. She would consider herself bipolar if she stopped to really think about her behavior.

Tristan saw the uncertainty in his mate's eyes as she pulled away from him and caught her wrist before she could move further away.

"Oh no you don't," he breathed out. "You don't get to just say that and then walk away Rhea."

Tristan used his grip on her wrist to drag her against his body and captured her mouth forcefully before she could protest. He groaned as he once again experienced her sweet taste and felt Rhea place her hands against his chest as he gently but determinedly coaxed her mouth open. All at once the kiss changed from forceful to frenzied. Tristan felt her respond to his aggression and he couldn't hold back anymore. He had his stunning mate in his arms and he could scent her arousal, turning him mindless with need.

Tristan grabbed the back of Rhea's thighs and hoisted her up so that she was pressed firmly against his aching cock. She whimpered at the sensation of him pressing against her core and shifted her hips to feel more friction even as his tongue wickedly dominated her mouth. Tristan growled and tightened his grip on her thighs as he carried her to his bedroom. He broke the kiss to place her on the centre of his bed and paused to relish the view of his mate lying in his domain where she belonged.

Tristan's nostrils flared as he inhaled Rhea's scent and he kicked off his shoes before climbing onto the bed to join his mate. She gazed at him with a sleepy sexy expression and whimpered as Tristan's body covered hers, effectively pinning her to the mattress. Tristan took her mouth again, this time slow and gentle. Rhea responded to his kiss by growing even wetter and she grabbed onto his shoulders to steady herself. She had never felt this all-consuming need before and if she had the ability to think clearly her mind would have been screaming at her to stop before things got out of hand.

Tristan ran his right-hand down Rhea's body as he kissed her, from her back down to her left thigh and held her firmly as he devoured her mouth. He felt Rhea move her hands down his chest timidly and growled as she reached the edge of his jeans. He removed his hand from her thigh and grabbed her hand that was against his lower abs, placing it firmly on his skin under his t-shirt and groaning at the feel of her skin on his. Rhea inched her hands slowly upward, feeling his warm skin under her palms and his firm abdominal muscles. She scraped her nails lightly against his skin and felt as well as heard him growl his approval.

Suddenly Rhea became aware of Tristan's hand lifting her t-shirt and she froze, memories she had buried coming to the surface in a great catastrophic rush. She whimpered again, this time in fear and pulled her hands away from him as if she had been scorched.

Tristan registered the sudden change in his mate and pulled away from her slowly, his heart breaking at the fearful expression in her eyes. He spoke softly to her, trying to get her to come back to the present.

"Rhea, Little One, its okay. You're safe. It's me, Tristan. Nobody is going to hurt you sweetheart," he cajoled gently.

Rhea heard Tristan's calm tender tone and was pulled back to where she was. She buried her face in his neck and sobbed as she recalled the images that had flown through her mind. She knew that she was safe with Tristan and felt so ashamed at her reaction, knowing that it would have hurt him badly as well.

Tristan was once again fuming as he realized that Rhea was terrified of intimacy. His wolf was nearly rabid with fury once again but his instinct to soothe and comfort his mate conquered his urge to rip apart the person who had caused her fear. He chastised himself for moving too fast and pushing her when she wasn't ready.

"I'm so sorry Tristan," she said, pulling backwards and startling him out of his chain of thought. "It wasn't you. I'm just so sorry."

Tristan kissed her cheek gently and brought her back into his arms.

"No my sweet, I'm sorry. I shouldn't have pushed you so fast," he breathed out.

"You are my mate. I will protect you for eternity, " Tristan promised.

"You know you're the only one I'm going to make love to," Rhea was got calm as Tristan reassured her.

Rhea's tiny cold hands pawed at Tristan's muscular broad. Rhea's skin was so sweet, so warm against his mouth. He needed more. He put his hands under her blouse, exploring her warm stomach and the faint outline of her ribs with his fingers.

Rhea moaned at his touch and impatiently pushed him away to shed her shirt, baring her lace encased breasts for him. He moaned in blissful agony seeing her show herself to him. He'd always loved Rhea, but he'd never realized how much it would turn him on and drive him insane to see her creamy mounds framed so delectably. His mouth traced her collarbone to her breastbone to rest between those soft mounds, delighting in the feel of her satiny skin against the sensitive flesh of his lips. He cupped one of her full breasts lovingly even as his mouth descended upon the other sucking at the taut nipple through the lacy fabric.

Rhea writhed and gasped beneath him whimpering in ecstasy even as her head thrashed back and forth on the sand. She was as beautiful as he'd imagined. Her whiskey-colored hair framing her face, her pale skin flushed with passion. He turned his attention to her other breast, pulling the lace away to bare her pink nipple that stood erect, waiting for him to suckle into his mouth. He latched onto it, hungrily suckling the tiny nub into his mouth, even as he reached behind her and unclasped the lacy bra. Now that he'd tasted her flesh, the beautiful lingerie only frustrated him.

Desperately Rhea began to undresshim, and he helped her, the same desire roaring through him to feel her warm, naked body against his skin. When their soft flesh finally met, an electric shock roared through his body. At long last he had someone. Rhea was so soft, so warm.

Full of passion and feral need, Tristan consumed Rhea's mouth again, mating his tongue with hers, groaning as her fingers traced the contours of his muscles and caressed his back. Those delicate hands seemed to be everywhere on his flesh, sending shivers of pleasure down his spine making his pulsing cock throb in agony. He groaned and pushed his pelvis into hers, the friction of their bodies teasing them both.

"Tristan," she gasped. She cried out as his mouth latched back onto one of her pink nipples and suckled, twisted and lathed it with hunger.

"Yes," he growled even as he continued to consume her flesh.

"Don't stop," Rhea ordered forcefully even as she raked his back with her nails.

"Never," he groaned as his mouth trailed downwards kissing the protrusion of her ribs and then making their way to her belly button.

His fingers nimbly undid her jeans and quickly pulled them from her hips, growling in desire at the thong that graced her mound. His mouth kissed the insides of her thighs and all around that small triangle of lace, making her jump as though his lips were shocking her with some kind of erotic electricity. He hungrily inhaled her musk even as he visually assessed her dampness, purring in satisfaction that he'd been the one to cause such passion. He latched his mouth to the fabric, tasting her arousal, smiling as she shrieked and twitched the moment his mouth made contact with her heat.

"Tristan," Rhea wailed in need. " Tristan..." she groaned.

Rhea's pleading cries shattered any control Tristan had left. He ripped the panties from her body and nearly lost it when he stared her glistening sex; shaved and hairless, red and weeping for his attention. He parted her folds and feasted on her, moaning into her softness at the sweet taste of her arousal.

Rhea screeched incoherently at his touch, whimpering with need, but he toyed with her, flicking her clit only for a moment before kissing or licking the juices that coated her.

Just before she cried out in frustration he'd suckle or nip her again, sending her beautiful head thrashing on the sand. Even as he licked and supped upon her sensitive flesh, he pushed a finger deep within her. He wanted to let Rhea know that she was his woman. She was Tristan's and Tristan's alone. He was going to take his time with her.

The heat was almost unbearable; her soft walls gripped his cock longingly. He inserted another finger and moved them within her slowly and gently at first, and then with more force and fervor. Her pelvis moved in tandem with his thrusts, her body coated his fingers with its juices, her hands balled up with need.

"Please," Rhea demanded, her voice hoarse from desperation. "Please Tristan."

Tristan looked up at her flushed body, her almost green eyes, her tousled hair and smiled at her. Taking pity on her, he latched his mouth over her clit suckling hard until she came screeching and bucking beneath him.

For a moment, he closed his eyes and took a deep breath struggling for control. It would be wrong to claim her. She didn't know his "dark secret." Still Tristan could hear the pounding of her heart, the blood throbbing in her sex, in the artery in her groin...

It took all of Tristan's control as he groaned in agony, forcing himself away from her weeping folds and back up her body delighting in the salty taste of her sweat, the musky scent in the air of her arousal.

Rhea reached out to run her fingers through his hair, those tiny fingers on his skin delighting his senses making his moans of need echo her own keening cries. His mouth supped its way up her neck, and back to her mouth, kissing her deeply, letting her taste herself on his lips. Suddenly she became more aggressive. With deft fingers, she unbuttoned his pants and put her hands inside to feel him.

Her soft hand wrapped around his cock stroking him, spreading the moisture of his arousal around the throbbing head with her thumb. It drove him insane to have her touching him while his body was imprisoned in his clothing.

Tristan's wolf growled impatiently and wanted only Rhea. He removed his pants and his boxers noting her wide-eyed stare with satisfaction. There was something about seeing her angelic eyes staring in amazement that nearly broke him and when she reached out once again and wrapped her slender fingers around him. He gasped in agony. It had been so long since he'd had a woman. Too long. For a moment all he could do was stare at that delicate hand wrapped around his throbbing erection and watch in mesmerized rapture as she stroked him. He groaned at her touch and closed his eyes for a moment as an image of her beautiful mouth devouring his cock flashed before his mind.

Not this time, he told himself.

Fearing to lose the last threads of control he took her tiny hand in his and held it still.

"Do you want this, Rhea?" he growled. Hoping against hope.

She didn't answer. Instead, she reached out with her other hand and pulled him down upon her again, kissing him passionately and forcing her tongue into his mouth.

He smiled at her unspoken demand. Even in bed she was stubborn and willful.

He kissed her with the same intensity, slipping his fingers back into her folds, stroking her sex, rubbing her clit, making her even hungrier for another release. In moments she was writhing beneath him again with need, both hands clinging to his shoulders as he assaulted her with his tongue and his questing fingers. When she was mindless with need, he took his impressive length in his hand and pushed it against her opening, slowly, trying to be mindful that her last penetration had been brutal. Whatever pain she'd last experienced he wanted to erase with pleasure.

They both groaned as he inched inside her. Tristan knew he was big for her. Still, Rhea was unbelievably tight around him, and he filled her so fully that they both lay still panting with the sensation. Tristan kissed her ear and then her lips. He worked his way down to her breast, suckling on her aching nipple. Rhea groaned and he felt her squirm beneath him. Then he started thrusting with agonizingly slow, steady strokes, watching himself disappear within her depths in rapt concentration.

She moaned beneath him and clasped his shoulders with her tiny hands, holding on as her body spun out of control with sensation.

"Tristan," Rhea moaned breathlessly. The pleading sound of his name on her lips sent a shiver down his spine.

He thrust harder even as he found every sensitive spot on her body with his fingers, making her writhe and squirm beneath him, smiling at his ability to fuel her passions so easily. She was beautiful in the throes of lovemaking and he wanted to watch her face as she came yet again at his expert touch. She whimpered and tossed her head from side to side, her fingers raked his back causing him to shudder deliciously, and in return he lightly twisted one of her hardened nipples making her squeak in bliss.

He slipped his hand between their bodies, flicking her clit as he thrust, earning a delicious whine from her lips and he watched in delight as he worked her into the frenzy of another orgasm. She came with a keening cry, her body convulsing beneath him, her sex gripping his cock. For a moment he almost lost control. However, in all his long years, Tristan had mastered the art of lovemaking. He wasn't ready to find his release yet. He had so much more pleasure to offer her with his body and his power.

She relaxed and nuzzled against him after she came down from her second orgasm, but he chuckled in her ear. "Oh no, my little love" he whispered in a dark, dangerous, masculine voice. "Our evening is far from over."

Rhea's eyes looked up at him uncomprehendingly. She could only coo in contentment as her response. Tristan growled possessively. This beautiful, delicate creature in his arms was HIS!

He began to kiss her hungrily then, his earlier tenderness turning to forceful passion. She obliged him, mating her tongue with his, suckling on it, nipping at his lips even as he nipped at hers. His hand palmed her breast and his hips began to thrust against hers again.

She groaned into his mouth as her body responded to his passion.

"You are mine, Little One," he growled in the language of the woods. "I am going to fuck you until your only thought is my body in yours. I'm going to make you scream my name in ecstasy."

Rhea didn't know what his words meant but whimpered at the sound of his dark, dominating voice. Her delicate fingers turned to claws as they raked down his back hungrily.

"That's it my little kitten," he continued. "I'm going to ignite the flames of your body like no man has ever done for you before. You're mine. MINE!"

Tristan felt his wolf start to morph. but he clenched his fist in her hair and with every last shred of his control he forced his beast down. Now was not the time for his dark secret. He wanted to pleasure Rhea. He didn't want to cause her alarm. Tristan focused on plundered her mouth once again, mating his tongue with hers fiercely and ground his hips against hers, stimulating her aching clit.

"And soon, little love," he growled, panting into her ear once again, "I'll claim your heart. I'll devour you and mark you as mine; my true mate. You are mine and no one else's.

She was gasping and moaning beneath him as he pounded her now. He took her legs in his arms and draped them over his shoulders groaning as he penetrated her dripping sex even deeper.

"Tristan" she cried as she built, her tiny claws drawing blood as they sunk deep into his muscular arms.

"You are MINE!" he growled into her ear.

This time her moan was a scream and her body convulsed beneath him, her tight walls gripping spasmodically around his cock. He came with the roar of his wolf, as he rode out their mutual orgasm.

Finally, as his breathing settled and her whimpers subsided, he caressed her hair from her face. Her eyes were closed, but he connected with her mind and felt her body still tingling with little shock-waves from her orgasm.

Soon enough Tristan's cock was hard again. He put it up against Rhea's pussy. He rubbed it around her lips making her moan his name in pleasure multiple times. He slipped his cock in only a few inches fucking her slowly before he moved a little faster going into her deeper. Soon enough Tristan was ready to cum in Rhea's tight pussy his cock pulsing and his balls getting those tingly sensations. Soon enough he was ready and he came into his mate, kissing her hard on the mouth.

"Are you all right?" Tristan whispered. Tristan was worried that he was too rough for her.

"Mmm," she replied in dreamy contentment and Rhea smiled up at her love.

"You are amazing, Rhea," he breathed, kissing her lips tenderly. "So incredible, I can't believe I've actually found you. You are not leaving my site anytime soon." he whispered. Tristan was delighted that Rhea was his.

For now, under the stars, Tristan was happy as his Rhea nuzzled against him in the warm afterglow. Rhea couldn't believe she felt so completely comfortable. Rhea wrapped her arms around Tristan. She closed her eyes and thought back to their love-making earlier. It was the best sex of her life- wild, erotic, passionate, and... she'd never had so many orgasms before. It had been a blissful day. Magical. What had happened between Tristan and her was beyond Rhea's wildest imagination.

Tristan nodded, not believing what he had longed for was coming true. He had a true mate. He had a true mate. He HAD a true mate. He drew Rhea into a deeper embrace and kissed her. He knew Rhea was his now.

THE END